PRODIGAL STORM

(TOCCATA SYSTEM, BOOK THREE)

KATE SHEERAN SWED

For my sisters.
Thanks for not being assassins.

1

———

LJ

Plymouthport, Eding

The Spyglass Tavern smelled like stale beer and saltwater, and LJ liked it that way. Fish stew bubbling in the background. Fresh-ish bread hardening on the counter. Holo vids babbling in the background with sports highlights and news updates on the hour, every hour.

Two weeks she'd been back here, each night worse than the previous. Two weeks since SATIS had forced her hand. LJ dipped her cloth in a tin of polish, her socks sticking to the tabletop as she stretched to reach the light fixture. The bar-bots could have been cleaning these for the last year while she'd been away, but no. SATIS hadn't bothered to program them to take care of real-life necessities.

For two weeks, LJ had scrubbed the Spyglass from floor to ceiling, but not only because of SATIS's maintenance failures. While LJ kept her hands moving, she could distract herself from the memories that plagued her every thought.

Because for two weeks, Conor Keyes's ghost had waited

on the other side of her dreams, haunting her nightmares and chastising her for her betrayal.

It was better to be awake. Which was why LJ was currently polishing chandeliers—if one could call them that —in the light of a dawn-fresh sky.

LJ reached for the top bolt on the fixture, and the table shuddered. She paused to regain her balance as voices clashed down the hall above, thundering steps creaking the old wood of the staircase and giving her a breath to prepare for their arrival.

Because LJ couldn't simply focus on banishing ghosts and invigorating the Spyglass's flagging business. No, on top of the haunted dreams and heart-shattering doubt that plagued LJ's days, Viv insisted on harboring these 'sisters' of theirs. Who *should* be able to move silently, and yet consistently chose to thunder instead.

Viv was LJ's true adoptive sister, the one she'd grown up with under SATIS's iron rule. LJ's mission was—and always had been—Viv's happiness.

"I saw the card in your cuff," one of the women said, accusing, as four of their 'sisters' landed in the room with the unconscious grace of cats. One with short, neon-green hair; one with a leather bracelet she never removed—the cuff in question, LJ supposed; one with a scar running from her nose to her chin, interrupting her lips along the way; and one who always smelled of rose perfume.

LJ was still working on names. "Weren't you having this argument when you went to bed?" she asked, kneeling to screw the top on the polish. Might as well get behind the bar and see if she could entice some customers into the place today.

"She cheated," Green-Hair said. "She forfeits her right to pick the first seat."

"Maybe *you* cheated," Rose Perfume said.

Thankfully, it didn't sound like the quartet were quite ready to start throwing punches. The unifying quality of Viv's rescues was that each and every one of them could kill with the flick of a pinky finger. It was part of what made them all SATIS's children; it was why, if not for Viv, LJ would've kicked them out long ago. And if the whole assassin thing weren't enough to test her, her 'sisters' glared at every stranger who ventured through the door, making business nonexistent. And they argued. A lot.

The quartet was still bickering as they headed for the back corner of the seating area, and LJ hopped down from her table, ready to intervene if necessary. She was more qualified to start fights than to stop them, but she'd promised Viv she'd keep an eye on things.

The women stopped in front of their usual table to face off. "Forfeit," Green-Hair commanded.

"I will not," Cuff responded, flipping blonde hair over her shoulder. Because you couldn't command a commander, apparently. "I won."

The women didn't have money to bet in a card game. Instead, they wagered bedroom positions, weapons, and, in this case, seating arrangements.

To anyone else, it would seem like a meaningless fight. But for an assassin, the person with her back to the corner could be the most powerful person in the room—and the least likely to take a bullet in the back. The women hid their anxiety behind walls of violence and posturing, but LJ saw the truth beneath the layers. They were afraid.

They should be. LJ had no clue what she was doing, and SATIS was gone.

She wished Viv would come home.

Cuff made her move, sauntering toward the corner with her hips swaying.

Green-Hair dove for Cuff, teeth bared, but LJ was ready; she grabbed the woman by her collar and shoved her against the wall, drawing her Edinburgh energy pistol out of its hip holster to aim at Rose Perfume—Cuff's clear ally, at least in this—and breathing deep to keep herself from slamming Green-Hair's head into the stone, her finger quivering on the pistol's trigger.

Because these women might be bad, but LJ was the worst of them all. None of them had committed anything approaching the horrors she'd been responsible for. If they knew the truth about her, even these supposedly cold-hearted killers would back away in terror.

But Viv wouldn't appreciate it if LJ killed one of her pets, even by accident. LJ nodded at Scar, the only one who hadn't participated in the fight. "You get the corner. No fighting."

LJ let go of Green Hair, who stared at her for a long moment, lip twitching, before giving her a brisk nod. LJ had no idea why they let her lead. Maybe they did know she was the worst of them. Or maybe because of Viv.

The women settled into their chairs as if nothing had happened, but tension still burned in the air. It would only get worse as the others woke and joined them. Only a matter of time before they erupted again.

LJ stalked across the bar, holstering the pistol and swiping the polish off the table to deposit it behind the bar. If Viv didn't come home soon, LJ was going to have to kill someone just to improve her mood.

Sighing, she pulled out a rag and wiped it across the perfectly clean counter, half an eye still trained on the burgeoning poker game. Even so, her split attention caught the creak of the stairs and the careful footsteps she recognized as Bethany's approach.

Bethany made it to the floor without falling and greeted LJ with a cheerful wave, but her bobbed brown curls were tangled around her face this morning, dark half-moons stamped beneath her eyes. LJ wasn't the only former assassin who hadn't been sleeping well.

"Lay a double on me, captain LJ ma'am," Bethany said, sliding onto her usual barstool at the end of the long counter. While a couple more assassins stepped out from behind her, beelining toward the corners, Bethany determinedly set her back to the door.

She wasn't an exception. She only pretended to be.

"You're gonna owe me for the finish on that stool," LJ said.

"Put it on my tab," Bethany said with a wink. "How about that double?"

The way she wobbled on her stool, she'd clearly already dipped into the flask this morning.

A shout erupted from the card game, and LJ flinched toward them before she realized the women were laughing. She lifted a bottle from the bottom shelf and poured two fingers into a glass, sliding it across the bar to Bethany, who accepted it with a salute. When LJ glanced over the counter, she could see the girl was still wearing her slippers. She'd considered trying to cut Bethany off, dry her out, but she couldn't quite convince herself it was the kind thing to do. Hell, she'd spent more than one night on that barstool herself since she'd been back, trying to drown the past while Conor's ghost laughed in her ear.

Bethany nodded to the holo vid, which was playing the news from its raised platform above the bar. "Can we put on a soap or something? I'm so sick of news I could vomit."

"Switch it to whatever," LJ said. "When a customer comes in, we'll change it back."

"Maybe you'd get one of those customer things you keep talking about, if you kept the soaps on all day. Or maybe a superhero movie."

"You a business owner?" LJ asked.

Bethany hiccupped. "No. But neither are you."

That, unfortunately, was true. Technically, SATIS owned the bar.

The door opened, and a knot LJ had been carrying in her chest for three days loosened. Viv had on her signature beret, gold hoop earrings shining against her dark brown skin. She came over to the bar and set down her suitcases.

"Huh," she said. "You kept them alive."

LJ hugged her, as best she could with the bar still between them. "Don't be so sure until you've counted."

The nature of Viv's assignments for SATIS had required gravity and socialization. So SATIS had raised LJ and Viv here in the Spyglass, together, as sisters. They were the lucky ones.

"Well, how'd it go?" Bethany said. "Find any more stragglers?"

Viv's eyes wandered to the game in the corner, as though she really were counting. She'd rounded up a dozen of them, with Viv and LJ making fourteen. Viv thought there were at least a dozen more to find. Plus a few, like Astra, whom Viv had never met.

LJ had met Astra, a couple of times. After *Traveler*, LJ didn't think they'd catch up with her again. She couldn't convince herself it was a bad thing. SATIS had forced LJ to finish the mission Astra wouldn't: kill Conor, because the AI jammer he'd invented made him too much of a threat.

Astra had taken one look at the AI jammer, at a chance

to be free of SATIS, and leapt at it. LJ hadn't had a choice, after that.

"I found another girl," Viv said.

"Where is she?" Bethany said. "Please tell me she was raised in a Maryan distillery. I'm dying for a sip of Quartian whisky."

"I didn't think your taste was so discerning," LJ said.

Bethany tsked. "Assumptions, assumptions, captain ma'am."

"Stop calling me captain," LJ said, but Bethany just grinned and mocked a toast.

Viv was still watching the game with one hand on the bar, eyes traveling to a girl in the corner by the fireplace, a pair talking by the window. Viv mothered them all. "She elected not to join us."

Ever since SATIS's voice had disappeared from their collective ears and nervous systems and been replaced, if briefly, by the dulcet tones of Edward Keyes, Viv had been on a mission to find the rest of SATIS's adoptees and bring them together on Eding. She'd been SATIS's real-world liaison, the AI's hands in a world the computer couldn't otherwise touch.

In other words, Viv knew where to look. She'd installed SATIS throughout the Toccata System herself. For some reason, Viv seemed to be convinced she'd had a choice in all that, and she refused to forgive herself for it.

LJ set a hand on her sister's shoulder and squeezed. "We can't expect to get them all."

Viv gave her head a little shake. "She's alone."

"Maybe she'll come around," Bethany said. When LJ gave her a surprised glance, Bethany just raised a shoulder. "What? I've got layers."

Viv traced a fingernail along the grain of the wooden

bar, brow furrowed. She didn't say anything else, but she didn't need to. She blamed herself for this, for all of it, but the responsibility was too big for one person.

All Viv had ever done was help them. She'd never even killed anyone.

"Not to interrupt your brooding," Bethany said as the holos started droning about current events, "but I thought we were going to change the channel."

As LJ turned back to tell her to control the holo from her tablet if she wanted to watch cheesy kissing vids so badly, the door opened again, wide enough this time for LJ to get a full view of the Plymouthport streets as the newcomer hesitated in the doorway. Plymouthport was a nighttime town—Eding was a nighttime *planet*, really—and streets hadn't yet begun to wake. The cleaning bots hadn't been out yet, and results of last night's revelries still puddled along the curbs.

Every night was a party on Eding's Archipelago.

"In or out," LJ said, the door still hanging open. "Smells great in here, don't need to change that."

The woman who walked in did not belong on Eding. She wore a neat pinstriped pants suit, tailored to fit her slim curves, and three-inch heels that were coated in mud. She carried a briefcase with shiny gold locks.

The woman approached the bar, retrieved a handkerchief from her pocket, and wiped the stool at the opposite end from Bethany before easing herself to sit. LJ watched her, amused, until she'd settled her briefcase beneath her feet.

"Can I get you a drink?" LJ asked.

The woman scanned the shelves, lips pursed. "Just water."

"That'll be twelve credits," Bethany said as LJ filled the glass and handed it across the counter.

"New to Eding?" LJ said as the woman stared at the water distastefully. She had no reason to. The Spyglass was clean, and if anything, LJ's determination to keep herself busy meant the glasses were triple washed. Daily.

"I am," the woman said. "Are you the owner of the Spyglass?"

LJ exchanged a glance with Viv. SATIS hadn't exactly left the bar behind in her will—or anything else—because SATIS hadn't made a will. It would've been a fake one, of course, but without their AI mother figure, they had no way to falsify documents or access bank accounts. Turned out rogue artificial intelligences didn't consider things like mortality.

"I'm the owner," LJ said. "And who are you?"

"I'm from Toccata Savings & Loan," the woman said.

Bethany snorted. "What'd you do to get transferred to Eding? Kill the boss's cat?"

The bank officer sniffed. "Ms. Havis, your payments to the bank are in default. Our attempts to contact you have gone unanswered."

Ms. Havis had been SATIS's favorite moniker. They'd searched for the accounts. They'd found nothing. And any messages would have gone unanswered because there was nothing to contact. SATIS was gone.

LJ cleared her throat. "I've recently run into some—"

"Let me be clear," the woman interrupted. "There is no room in your contract for late payments.

"Not even after years of perfect billing?" Viv asked.

The woman blinked at her. "She hasn't had years of perfect billing. Her payments have been erratic at best. The past six months have been a disaster as far as the bank is concerned."

SATIS had only been gone for a few weeks. She'd

survived Conor by less than a day, measured by the timing of Keyes's message. What would have happened, if SATIS had disappeared before? But no. There was no point in harping on the past.

The banker was shuffling her things around, preparing to leave. Before LJ could formulate a response—or figure out how to beg—the tavern door banged open for the third time in fifteen minutes.

LJ hadn't met the woman whose silhouette darkened the doorway, but she recognized the stance. A SATIS daughter. Razor thin and black-haired, the newcomer stood with her shoulders back, feet hip-width apart, energy practically pulsing through her limbs as she prepared to spring forward. A six-inch blade glinted in her hand.

Before LJ could move, the woman rushed into the room, aiming her knife at Viv's throat.

Using the storage shelf under the bar for leverage, LJ leapt across the counter as Bethany toppled off her stool to knock Viv out of the way. Surprisingly good reflexes.

The attacker's knife sank into the wooden bar top, and the bank woman screeched. LJ hardly heard her as Viv's attacker whipped back around, ready to fight. She had ebony hair pulled into a bun behind her head, pale white skin, and eyes brimming with rage.

The poker players tipped over tables and chairs as they rushed across the room, but they might as well have been running in slow motion. Viv's attacker moved, fluid-fast, and LJ grabbed her by the wrist, trying to twist. The woman anticipated her and broke the hold, throwing a punch, but LJ was faster. She intercepted and blocked a second punch, forearm registering the force of the blow as she landed her own hit to the assassin's nose. Blood streamed from the woman's nostrils, but she didn't even pause. Given a breath, she reached for her boot, and LJ knew that she couldn't let the woman reach whatever weapon she'd hidden there.

She jabbed the assassin in the hip with her knee, then hit her already-gushing nose a second time when she stumbled. Blood coated LJ's fist as the woman screamed, in anger or pain or both, and LJ whirled to rip the knife out of the bar. Before her opponent could even cough the blood out of her sinuses, LJ was facing her again. She kicked the woman in the hip a second time and took out her left knee, forcing her to the floor.

LJ was vaguely aware of someone—Viv?—calling her name, but everything was muted against the rushing beat of blood in her ears. She pinned Viv's attacker with her knee, hit the woman in the eye for good measure, and pressed the blade against her throat, bracing herself against the floor, palm tacky with blood.

The woman froze, her eyes still wild. For half a second, LJ considered ending this right now. It would be so easy. The knife quivered against its owner's skin, hungering for a kill. With the whitewater rush of adrenaline pouring through her veins, LJ nearly gave in. The only thing that stayed her hand was the thought of Viv's face, and how disappointed she would be.

"Who are you?" LJ said. "Tell me fast, and I'll kill you fast."

The woman spat in her face. LJ lifted a hand to hit her again, but someone caught her arm from behind, pulling at her as though to drag her away. LJ maintained her grip against the shift in balance, pressing the back of the blade against the woman's skin. "Who. Are. You?"

"Lemme guess," Bethany said, kneeling beside the woman's head. "You're the one who elected not to join us."

"LJ. Let go," Viv said.

LJ did not intend to do any such thing. This woman had

gone straight for Viv, and she knew how to fight. If LJ let her go, this stranger could tear Viv apart with her bare hands. LJ had paid too much to lose Viv like that.

In all her years of fighting, LJ had hesitated exactly once. She knew the cost. She wouldn't do it again. In her years of chasing down targets, she'd never met anyone who fought like this, in the same quick, concentrated movements she'd been trained for. If anything, LJ thought, this assassin had gone down a little too easily.

On the floor, the woman sneered. "Aren't you all a nice little family? I don't suppose Viv told you anything about what happened to SATIS, either, but here you are, all cozy. For all we know, Viv killed our mother."

LJ had been with Viv when SATIS went silent, when Edward Keyes's voice interrupted that silence to inform them that SATIS was dead. And to put in a request of his own, as if any of them would drop everything they'd been taught to join him. The man was delusional.

And so was this one. Whose name LJ didn't know, and would probably forget as soon as she learned it.

"Viv doesn't know what happened to SATIS," LJ said.

"Don't be thick. She knows *everything*. She's the liaison. She's the... the..."

"Accomplice," Viv said quietly.

"You said it, not me."

For a moment, everyone was quiet. Then a soft voice said, "Maybe if LJ will give her some space, we can talk."

LJ hadn't noticed Sophie. She didn't know many of their names, but if Viv mothered everyone, then everyone mothered Sophie. She was the youngest of them, barely eighteen, with a wispy quality that made her seem timid and fragile. As if the slightest wind might dissolve her.

And yet she'd left her reading corner to join the group in the middle of the fight, though she placed herself at the edge. It was hard to picture the soft-spoken girl as an assassin. Maybe she'd done more spying than killing. Maybe SATIS had considered her a dud. It happened.

LJ didn't move. "She didn't come here to talk. Did you?"

"Not to you."

Amazing, really, that it hadn't come to this before now. All these former assassins forced together with nothing to do but wait? LJ was supposed to be the one preventing the violence while Viv was away, but her sister should have known better. They were all fighters, but LJ... LJ might have been born to it.

And it was Viv's gaze that brought her back from the brink now. LJ dropped the knife and let her sister pull her away, and a couple of the poker players hauled the newcomer to her feet. The woman's eyes still flashed, but the fight had gone out of her. She dabbed at her nose with a napkin, a strangely prim motion compared to the rest of her.

LJ moved back to stand beside Bethany.

"You know," Bethany said, "I might not be handling my trauma so well, but at least I'm handling it."

LJ rubbed her wrist. "What's that supposed to mean?"

"Oh, nothing. Just for a second, I thought you were going to kill that one. Like you were still working for *her*, or something."

Bethany didn't even like to name SATIS. How was that handling her trauma? Viv knew the other girls' stories, but she treated them with confidential respect. If LJ knew anything about what they'd endured in their roles as SATIS minions, it was because they'd volunteered it.

Bethany hadn't volunteered anything but jokes and

drink orders. At least LJ was trying to rebuild her life, while Bethany drank hers away.

LJ commanded her own destiny now. She was fine.

The bank woman pushed past the group of assassins, her hair frizzed at the edges. She set her briefcase on the stool beside LJ, opened the clasps with a businesslike *click!*, and shoved a paper at LJ with trembling hands. "You have a week to pay your balance in full," she said, pointedly not looking at the blood that was now spattered across the floor. Apparently banks turned the other way when it came to violence, as long as the bills were paid. "Good luck with that."

Casting one last disgusted look around the Spyglass, the bank woman stalked out toward the street.

"Huh," Bethany said, "I forgot she was here. And she didn't drink her water. Rude."

LJ crumpled the paper in her hand and tossed it back behind the bar. It didn't matter if she owed ten credits or ten thousand. She couldn't pay it.

The sound of the news floated above the lull, an on-the-hour update they'd seen replayed a few hundred times by now: Edward Keyes, the man they'd been raised to despise, sitting before the Toccata System Council, his smooth baritone voice arguing for control over AIs on Eding so he could install some kind of patch.

LJ would be the first to admit the need, but Keyes shouldn't be the one to do it. He'd been the one to program love into SATIS, the kind that decimated AI protocol for the sake of her beloved. Which was part of the reason Conor had invented the jammer to begin with.

All of SATIS's adoptees were staring at the holo, even the new girl. Staring at Edward Keyes. The sight of him rolled LJ's stomach, but for different reasons. They'd all been raised to hate him, but only LJ had to turn away. Because Edward Keyes looked like his son.

Instead of watching him, LJ made herself look at Viv. Her sister studied the holo, fidgeting with her earring and glancing at the girls as though to gauge everyone's reaction so she could slip into the role of counselor at a moment's notice if they needed her.

SATIS had forced LJ to choose between Conor and Viv. Had LJ not killed him, Viv would be dead. The fact had no impact on the ghost that haunted her every time she closed her eyes, but it was the truth, and LJ refused to forget it. Viv's guilty conscience might call her to martyr herself at the altar of the AI's evil schemes, but it was SATIS who'd done the killing. LJ was just a tool.

Conor haunted her dreams because she *missed* him. She forced herself awake, not because she felt guilty, but because she didn't want to face the reminder that he was gone. Now, here, Keyes was an older version of Conor's ghost—one she couldn't banish so easily. Even his voice sounded like Conor, and LJ had to squeeze her eyes shut against the ache in her throat.

"This is why I wanted to change the channel," Bethany said, and LJ forced her eyes back open as Rose Perfume punched a fist through Keyes's hologram head.

"Wait," Viv said. "It's different this time."

Sure enough, a new voice was speaking over the footage. The holo cut to a man dressed in an expedition outfit that was so pristine he might have been modeling it for a zine. He had on round spectacles and a hat that looked designed for safari. The interviewer introduced him as Parker Trelawney.

"I'm heading to Eding as we speak," Trelawney said, his accent as affected as it was excited. "I've been granted exclusive access to the island where Edward Keyes will be doing his momentous work, and I'll be returning with in-depth information on his plans for Toccata's AIs."

"Live?" the interviewer asked.

Trelawney presented a practiced laugh. "If Keyes's shut-down allows for it."

Diplomatic as he was, LJ interpreted that as a solid 'no.' Trelawney clearly wanted to spin the story, not allow it to develop. But why?

"I know we're all eager to know more about what Edward Keyes has planned," the faceless interviewer said. "After the events of the last month, action seems necessary."

The events of last month. First, SATIS had infiltrated *Traveler*'s AI system, somehow, wreaking havoc across the ship in a short-lived battle that ended with her disappearance. LJ had been halfway back to Eding when the *Traveler* news broke, but it seemed impossible that it could have been a coincidence. And for Landry City's AIs to go haywire the following week... It almost felt planned.

LJ had a feeling it was Edward Keyes who needed to be shut down. Not the AIs. Oh, the computers still needed patching—but only to stop the Keyes-es of the world from enacting their evil plans.

"Mr. Keyes certainly convinced the council, but I'd like more information," Trelawney said, and LJ liked the reporter a hair more. "That's why I'm going."

"When will you arrive?"

"As soon as I secure travel arrangements, I'll be on my way. I'm heading to Eding to book passage to his island."

"I suppose you won't give us a hint about where that is?"

Trelawney gave the laugh again. "Sorry. Nondisclosures, etcetera."

"Well. I'm sure I speak for everyone in the system when I say we wish you well and look forward to your report."

"Tally ho," Trelawney said. "I'll be in touch."

Trelawney blinked away, and the vid flipped back to a replay of Keyes before Bethany picked up her tab and stabbed the screen with a finger to make him disappear.

For a beat, they all looked around at each other. And for one moment, LJ saw them for what they were: strangers, most of them barely past twenty, lost and orphaned. Even the new girl, whoever she was. Someone had taken SATIS from them, and it was hard to see that as a bad thing; but the man SATIS had raised them to hate had plans for the system, and that was a problem.

If LJ hadn't known Conor—one day she'd think of him without her stomach tying itself into painful knots—she might have thought SATIS's villainy canceled Keyes's. The truth was, what he'd done to SATIS was only the beginning. Conor had described, in detail, how Keyes had used his creations in the intervening years, pushing them beyond the edge of corruption and taking lives in the process.

Not to mention that he'd tried to recruit SATIS's children to his current cause, whatever it was.

"If he's going to mess with the AIs on Eding," Viv said slowly, "does that mean we might be able to use them to access SATIS's archives? Our accounts?"

And keep the Spyglass stuttering along until they made a profit again. Without that, Viv couldn't take care of the girls. Which meant LJ couldn't take care of Viv.

It was the new girl who spoke first. "I don't know about you," she said, "but I've got a ship."

LJ turned to evaluate her. Scar and Green-Hair still held her by the arms, but it hardly seemed necessary; Keyes's appearance had taken the fight out of them all. The girl met her gaze with calm consideration. Not a friend, but maybe an ally. "What's your name?" LJ asked finally.

The other woman smiled, then winced and touched her still-bleeding nose. "Maybe we can make a deal after all, if it's an anti-Keyes one," she said. "I hate him as much as you do. I'm Fay."

3

CONOR

Two Days Later

When Conor's pod touched down on Eding, he half expected it to miss the dock and crash into the water. The spaceport jutted off the island in a jangle of metallic limbs, and though his ship was cleared to land at any available dock, he couldn't see how that would be possible without requiring him to swim.

Conor was in no shape to swim.

At least he'd managed to snag his own ship after he regained consciousness and fled *Traveler*'s medical bay. His ship-to-ground pod relied on pre-programmed landing specs instead of the AI pilot most people used. Still, he didn't like to rely on any machine for his safety. As soon as the hatch hissed open, he unbuckled the straps and lifted his body carefully out of the seat.

He would have run from the ship, but he was in no condition for that, either. He was lucky to be alive at all.

Easily distinguishable among the muted fashions of the

Archipelago's citizens, Parker Trelawney raised his hand in a wave as Conor navigated his way across the short bridge to the pier, using the cane he'd swiped from *Traveler*'s infirmary to help him keep his balance. It was amazing how weak he felt, with half of his abdominal muscles sliced through the middle, his stomach stitched, his ribcage grazed.

Not to mention the two weeks he'd lost to a medically induced coma—according to the intel he'd asked Parker to gather for him, since Conor had conveniently left *Traveler* before consulting with any medical staff. The Star Leaders Academy ship had still been reeling after the hijacking of its central AI, an incident Conor had missed entirely; no doubt it was tied to Astra Havis and the rogue AI that had raised her.

Confusion or no, he doubted he'd have been able to escape when he'd woken—not quite two weeks after the hijacking—had the feed of his father speaking to the council about AI patches not been playing across the ship. Ironic, that. While everyone had been distracted by Edward Keyes's supposed plans to save them, Conor had hobbled through the ship and slipped away.

Conor hadn't asked how Trelawney had accessed *Traveler*'s medical data. He hoped it involved networking and favors rather than AI assistance. In addition to the coma, which was alarming enough, Conor had apparently died on the table for nearly a minute during the period of time that *Traveler*'s AI was compromised. No heartbeat, no oxygen, no hope.

No Laura. Questions pounded through his mind whenever she entered it, beating in time with his wound. Where was she? Had she been working for Astra's AI? He didn't want to believe she'd been working for his father—that

would undermine his entire reason for coming to Eding—
but he couldn't rule it out, either.

And why? his wound pulsed in question. *Why, why, why
had she betrayed him?* When he'd thought... Well. It didn't
matter what he'd thought.

Now, he had to fight the urge to hunch over and protect
his healing stomach as he made his way slowly to his friend.
The dock was a mishmash of circular landing pads and
docked ships, with no apparent pattern in the design. The
Archipelago's aesthetics certainly fit its reputation for
unruliness. Though how a place could be unruly when it
had few actual rules was beyond his understanding.

Conor stepped over a short gap between the landing pad
bridge and the pier, his wound protesting sharply as he
maneuvered across it. He probably should've stayed in the
hospital for another day, or ten, but he hadn't been able to
shake the sensation that if he'd stayed, someone would
return to finish the job Laura had left undone.

Thank goodness for canes. This one was simply black,
functional, with a curved handle and rubber on the bottom.
It kept him standing upright. It kept him moving forward.
Without it, he felt fragile.

When Conor set two feet safely on solid ground,
Trelawney came over to clap him on the shoulder. He had
on a blinding white outfit with about twelve visible pockets.

"My god, Parker," Conor said, "what the hell are you
wearing?"

Trelawney beamed. "Like it? If I'm going to be an
explorer, I need to play the part."

Conor groaned. "Please tell me you're being discrete."

After he'd woken from his coma to the sound of his
father buttering up the System Council, Conor had called
his reporter friend—from his ship, of course—to offer him

exclusive guidance to Edward Keyes's hideout on Eding, if Trelawney would arrange transportation.

"As discrete as an ace reporter can," Trelawney said, winking.

Not at all, then. Great. If Trelawney had alerted old Eddie to the plan, they'd be deep in shit before they'd even left Plymouthport.

"This isn't my usual type of story," Parker said. "I was halfway to the Canon System when you called."

For all his flash, Trelawney was more of a war correspondent than anything else. The Toccata System might be peaceful, for the most part, but neighboring systems like Canon had a tendency to erupt. Conor had known his friend would understand the request for what it was: an SOS. "I appreciate the cover," Conor said.

Trelawney shrugged, like it was no big deal. But he'd come, when Conor had no one else. "Got any bags?" Parker asked.

Conor shook his head. "Left in a hurry."

He was going to need to pick up a change of clothes. Looking around, he thought he'd be lucky to find something to wear that didn't have a skull and crossbones decal across the chest. Or worse.

As Trelawney led him through the streets, Conor could almost imagine people staring at them. Of course, that could have been the way his friend was dressed; Parker might as well have painted a ROB ME sign on the back of that horrific beige outfit.

Plymouthport was bustling with people, and though Conor wasn't generally one to judge, not many of them looked particularly savory. Sailors clustered around fast running schooners, smoking cigarettes and arranging themselves a bit too casually around crates that probably contained every controlled substance in the system. Hover-carts drifted along the street, electronic voices calling wares to a crowd that did not appear to have the credits to buy anything.

As Conor and Trelawney moved away from the port, the crowd grew thicker and rowdier, people jostling by Conor and making him wince with every step. Loud laughter and crashes echoed out of taverns, more than one door spilling brawlers into the dirt as Conor and Trelawney passed. The smell of fish and stale urine mixed in the growing heat, with sweat and saltwater drifting along on top. Conor placed his cane carefully to avoid the frequent puddles that were too putrid to be rain.

"I got you the ship of your dreams, my man," Trelawney said, strolling along as though they were out for a walk in a park. He didn't seem bothered by Eding's melee. "Found this girl who's lived here on the Archipelago her whole life. She's a treasure. She's taking care of it all."

Conor wasn't sure if he was ready to trust anyone who'd lived on Eding her whole life, let alone this corner of it. The Archipelago was a crescent of islands seeded along Eding's southern hemisphere and it was, if the cultural competence classes he'd bothered to attend at the Star Leaders Academy could be believed, as lawless as a place could get. It had the reputation, and even in broad daylight Conor had to fight the urge to keep a hand on his tablet to make sure it stayed in his pocket.

To be fair, though, Conor wasn't sure if he was ready to trust anyone ever again, regardless of where they hailed from. Even trusting Parker felt like a stretch, and Parker was nothing if not loyal.

Edward Keyes's treachery had never robbed Conor of his faith in people; despite everything, he'd believed in humanity's inherent goodness, even if it landed him in trouble more than once. But Laura's betrayal had cut through more than flesh.

"As long as the ship is free of AIs, it sounds great," Conor said.

"No ship is," Trelawney said, "unless you designed it, friend. But we're doing it old school like you asked, across the big blue sea. Your dad won't see us coming."

Conor sighed. He supposed it was too much to ask to secure a vessel that didn't require an AI to run. A rowboat would have been preferable. He wished he hadn't lost his jammer, or had had the ability to make a new one.

No use dwelling on that, though. He wished a lot of things. The physical pain of the last few days had taken most of his mental energy, but in the quiet moments, he could only think of Laura. He didn't want to replay those final moments in his head, or imagine how she must have been laughing at his foolish question. Worse, he didn't want to replay the year that had come before her betrayal. He didn't want to talk himself into believing anything between them had been real.

Because it wasn't. Laura had killed him. The end. It didn't matter why. It didn't matter where she'd gone.

Only one thing mattered, and it was this: that the moment Conor had seen his father on the news holos talking about Eding, he'd known that Dad would use his old lab to shut down the AIs. And then he'd do everything he could to make sure the Toccata System's AIs served him, and him alone. The council might not even know it for years, and by then there'd be no way to untangle themselves.

Conor would get to the island. He'd let old Eddie shut down the AIs—it had to happen, to install the patch. But Conor would make sure they stayed that way.

Once upon a time, he hadn't thought AIs were a problem at all. He'd seen himself following in his father's footsteps, leading the system in progress and innovation.

Conor didn't have a mother, or at least, he hadn't been raised with one. But his father had allowed him into every conversation, took him along on every business trip. Which was why, when Conor was fourteen, old Eddie had thought nothing of taking his son on a visit to the power mines he'd recently acquired in the center of Toccata's asteroid belt.

The mine had been tucked into an asteroid beyond Orthos, the surface too cold to support life and yet crawling with it, the inside so over-mined that people had to descend for a full day to reach mineable resources. By system standards, Conor learned later, the asteroid had been a month or two from going out of service, the conditions too unsafe to sustain.

On the surface, miners had lived in basic domes, huddling around heaters barely warm enough to keep them alive. When they'd descended for their weeklong shifts, they'd left letters for their families, trading packets of last words back and forth as a matter of course.

That alone had been enough to horrify Conor. But then, while he'd been there, a power rupture had killed fifteen miners in one explosion, trapping another dozen. There'd been no way to save them.

But the worst part was the way the miners on the surface had reacted. They'd hardly blinked at the news, simply fishing out the proper letters and designating someone to send them. It'd been an expectation. A matter of when, rather than if.

So Conor had designed a solution. Over a week of sleepless nights, he'd programmed SimuBot, an AI that analyzed data and mining patterns to choose the safest places to work and recommend timelines for abandoning the mine altogether. Conor had understood the material risk well enough; his father might lose money. He'd assumed his father would understand.

Looking back, Conor tried to think of himself as charmingly naive. Because of course, of *course*, Edward had found a way to corrupt Conor's invention into a power-seeking machine, using it to slip around Toccata regulations until he'd chipped every mineable resource out of the rock. And as the asteroid had given up its final riches, the whole thing'd caved in, breaking into millions of pieces and killing hundreds of workers.

But Edward couldn't have known it would do that. He might have manipulated the code—that was his way—but SimuBot should have outlined how to save the miners before the asteroid died, and not just the precious commodity. At first, Conor'd assumed his own coding had been to blame. But no matter how he studied the problem, the final twist always came back to the computer. Whether SimuBot had misinterpreted Edward's wishes, or simply gone its own way, Conor had never been able to discover.

There were no safe AIs in Toccata, or anywhere. If Conor could solve Toccata's AI problem—really solve it—and if he could redeem his father in the process... Maybe he'd finally be able to redeem himself, too. Designing that AI might have been among his first mistakes, but it certainly hadn't been his last.

He'd thought it was enough to invent a jammer, but that hadn't even protected his life, let alone the whole system. A clean slate. It was the only way.

Laura wasn't a factor. Not anymore. "When do we leave?" he asked.

"Tomorrow morning. Come meet our travel guide," Trelawney said. "You're gonna like her. I promise."

What Conor really wanted was a bed and a good night's sleep, but as that was unlikely in any case, he supposed it would be a good idea to check Trelawney's work. "Where is she?"

"She owns a tavern a few streets over," Trelawney said. "It's called the Spyglass."

$$4$$

LJ

L J wasn't sure what all should be stocked in the kitchen of a ship, but starting with bread could never be a bad idea. While the others were scurrying around with shopping lists and duffel bags, she stood at the tavern's kitchen counter with her hands knuckle-deep in dough. Bread made sense to her. Cooking made sense to her. When something went wrong, it came down to human error, faulty ingredients, or malfunctioning cookware.

Simple. Emotion-free.

She wasn't avoiding the others, not exactly, but Viv's presence temporarily relieved her from babysitting duty. Of course, Viv was staring her down in the kitchen at the moment, but her sister would deal with any eruptions from the common room, if they arose.

Not that LJ was avoiding anyone.

"Are we sure we want to do this?" Viv asked. She was leaning back on the stove, and LJ wanted to tell her to be careful not to flick the burners on by mistake. Viv had delicate rows of rhinestone-studded hoop earrings trailing up her ears today, her nails bright with ruby-red polish. She'd somehow managed to make time for everyone in the two days since she'd been back—Viv didn't need clipboards or lists to remember their names—and LJ didn't know how her sister was even standing.

"You want to keep up your find-the-assassins game, right?" LJ said, and Viv nodded. "Then if you want them to have a place to sleep, yes. The reporter needs a ship to get to Keyes's island, and the AIs. We have one."

There. She could say the name. If it stuck in her throat a little, at least it hardly hurt. She was getting better at the whole numb thing. She really was. She breathed in the scent of the kitchen, yeast and herbs, wood and hops. It was better than meditation. It kept her hands moving.

Viv dug the toe of her sandal along a crack in the floor. The sole was lifting away from the bottom. She needed new ones. "Intercept Keyes, take control of the AIs, access our accounts, save the Spyglass."

LJ punched the bread. "Exactly."

Viv gave her an is-that-all roll of her eyes, but she didn't protest. "And the reporter fell for your pitch?"

"Hook, line, sinker."

Viv kept toeing at the crack. She had something else to say, so LJ waited. "But what are we going to do about Keyes's plans for the system?"

LJ shrugged. Once they had access to their accounts, she didn't care what happened. But convincing Viv to stop trying to save everyone would be like convincing the waves to stop rolling, so LJ said, "If we take the code for ourselves we'll be saving the system, too. Like a side effect."

"Do you mean silver lining?"

"Whichever cliched metaphor works best." She nearly cringed as the words left her mouth; it was a Conor thing to say, but she bit her tongue and kept kneading.

Viv ran a finger along the hoops in her left ear, clearly unconvinced.

LJ's tab lit up with a message, and she leaned over the counter to read it. *Fancy pants reporter guy is here. Fancy purple pants, specifically. Also he brought a friend. -Beth*

LJ sighed and abandoned her dough for the moment, wiping her hands on a towel before stepping out of the kitchen, with Viv right behind her. The tavern was relatively empty, with everyone out gathering supplies and helping Fay to prepare the ship. Whatever that entailed. Bethany sat on her usual stool, spinning a bar glass.

LJ planted a finger on top of the glass to stop it from toppling off the bar. "You couldn't have walked three steps to tell me Trelawney's here?"

Bethany blinked. "But then I'd have to get up."

"Oh, shit," Viv said.

LJ looked at her sister, startled. Viv was staring out into the tavern, eyes wide, lips parted in shock. Viv had worked with assassins her whole life. She'd shepherded a newly made cyborg into SATIS's care—they hadn't found that one yet—and infiltrated prisons, smuggling rings, and the dregs of the system, all in the service of finding appropriate orphans for SATIS's care.

It was difficult to shock Viv. LJ followed her sister's gaze across the tavern.

Trelawney sat at a table in the center of the room, smiling amiably. His default expression, judging from their brief video calls. He looked as out of place in the dingy tavern as a diamond in a manure pile, but at least he was happy about it.

Sitting beside him was Conor Keyes. Not an apparition, nor a phantom. Conor. He was alive.

LJ's chest burned, then froze over. She could feel the

knife in her hand as it entered his flesh, the shock in his eyes, the heat of his blood soaking into her shirt. The way he fell.

Marry me, Lor.

He was supposed to be dead.

LJ set a hand on the bar to steady herself. He hadn't seen her yet. He was reading something on his tab with rapt attention, strands of sandy hair dipping across his forehead. He looked thin. Pale. But alive. A dozen options unfolded in her mind—retreat to the kitchen, run for the door, leap over the bar and finish it before SATIS could hurt Viv—but her body refused to obey her commands. Her feet might have been fused to the floor.

Her training faltered and drained away.

Bethany looked back and forth between LJ and Viv, then over at the table where the men were sitting.

Viv licked her lips. "Maybe I should..." she began, then stopped, because it was too late.

Conor looked straight at them.

He stood abruptly, his chair crashing to the floor behind him. The movement cost him, and he flinched, shoulders rounding briefly as Trelawney rose, his smile fading into concern as he offered his arm for support. Conor didn't look at his friend. He braced a hand on the table, keeping his gaze locked on LJ. Just like the ghost from her dreams. Only the living Conor's skin was flushed with the effort of standing—with fear too, LJ thought with a pang of electric feeling she couldn't begin to sort—his gray-green eyes all too alive.

So this was how Trelawney knew the location of Keyes's secret island. He was working with Conor. Who was back from the dead.

"Laura," Conor said. She thought he'd have run for the

door, if he could have. But she knew where she'd stabbed him. There was no way he could run. He shouldn't be here at all.

LJ forced herself to breathe. He was staring at her, his knuckles gripping bone-white on the edge of the table, like he expected her to launch into a full explanation of her actions. Or attack him.

With an effort, LJ unclenched her jaw. "No one calls me Laura," she said, because she had to say *something*, and there was nothing else in her mind. Everything was hot and cold and blank, the present flickering with the past until she thought she might black out.

Conor gave her a half smile, his eyes cold. He didn't have to say it. He'd spent a year calling her Laura while she guarded his movements and sent intel back to SATIS so Astra could break his heart. When LJ closed her eyes, she could still hear him whispering her name in the darkness.

When SATIS had learned about Conor's jammer, she'd shifted her plans overnight, from heartbreak to murder. Or so LJ had thought, until today.

At the bar, Bethany set her glass down. "This is intense. Way better than a drama vid. They slept together, right? I feel like they slept together."

"No," Viv said, but she didn't sound certain, and LJ didn't dare meet her sister's eyes. If she did, Viv would know what LJ had managed to hide from everyone but SATIS.

"Why'd you do it, Lor?" Conor said. He was using the old nickname intentionally, she could tell. His tone, though. His tone was ice. They might have been alone in the bar, the others blurred to shades of mist. "Money? Status? Pure bloodlust?"

He was mocking her, she knew that, and she shouldn't let him. But words shriveled on her tongue, her throat dry.

Bethany said, "Wait, is this the Academy guy you killed? Elj, I don't think he's dead."

LJ swallowed, flailing for her training, for some semblance of calm. "I've killed a lot of guys." Her insides might be slowly breaking apart, but at least her voice sounded steady. She could only hope her expression was equally casual. "Stop looking at me like that, Conor. My orders ran dry. Besides, if I kill you now, I'll have to kill him, too."

She pointed to Trelawney, whose already owl-like eyes widened further. He really was wearing purple pants.

"Who gave those orders?" Conor said. "Was it my father? Or Astra's AI?"

LJ didn't want to tell him. She wanted him out of her bar. They'd have to find another way to Keyes; Conor would never travel with them, and even if he somehow decided to trust her, LJ would spend every night awake in her bed waiting for him to try and murder her in her sleep.

And then she'd be forced to kill him. Again.

"Ding ding ding, mama AI for the win," Bethany said from the bar, lifting her empty glass in a fake cheers. "Jammer boy wins the prize."

So much for keeping their secrets. For the first time, Conor looked at Bethany. His gaze traveled to Viv, and to the stream of activity as the others ran in and out on errands. As different as they were, the women moved like lithe soldiers, muscles identifying them easily to anyone who knew what they were looking for. She could see him putting the pieces together. He'd always been smart that way.

"Your father's AI," LJ reminded him. "Not Astra's."

"The AI raised all of you?" Conor said, incredulous. "Astra didn't mention that."

"Astra didn't know," Viv said. "SATIS liked to...experiment."

"She's gone now," Bethany said, twirling on her barstool. "We don't know where."

Trelawney looked like his eyes were about to pop out of his skull and roll across the floor. "I'm confused."

LJ snorted a laugh. "He probably dragged you into this without telling you a goddamn thing."

"All I want is a clear road to Edward Keyes," Trelawney said, but the way he watched Conor made LJ think that was less than the truth.

"A clear patch of sea, you mean."

Fay. She stood in the doorway with a box in her arms, because LJ was cursed and the person who already mistrusted her—she had the broken nose to prove it—just had to be here to witness the revelation of LJ's number-one weakness. Fay propped the box on the bar and gave them a questioning look.

Conor took another step back from the table, covering his wince quickly with a hand to his forehead. "No," he said, when he'd stabilized. Conor had never worried about rushing things. He gave himself the time he needed. "We'll find another way. Goodbye, Laura."

Using a cane for support, Conor walked to the door without looking back, his friend hovering by his elbow.

Good. That was good. It was better if they left.

"No one calls her Laura," Bethany called after him. "How come no one calls you Laura, by the way? What's the J stand for? Are we stopping the preparations?"

LJ ignored her. Bethany shrugged and poured another finger of whisky into her glass.

Viv straightened away from the bar. "Something you want to tell me?"

LJ tucked her fingers into her pockets. "Not really." She should be terrified, horrified at her failure. Instead she just felt... thawed. Like all the numbness and horror of the past two weeks was draining away. It didn't matter if she never saw him again. If any bastard in the world could survive a wound like that, it was Conor. He lived, he breathed, and she wanted to collapse in the corner and sob with the relief of it.

She couldn't. Not with the others here, with Fay watching. That one would strike as soon as she sniffed out a weakness.

Viv leaned closer, her expression all concern. "Come on, LJ. All this time you two were...and then SATIS made you..." She shook her head. "Did SATIS know?"

Of course SATIS had known. LJ'd tried to hide it, and SATIS had even let her believe she'd succeeded. Until the AI pieced together the truth about Conor's jammer, at which point she'd felt threatened enough to want him off the board.

There's more than one way to break Edward Keyes's heart, SATIS had said when she'd transmitted LJ's adjusted orders.

Zap me in the temple all you want, LJ had responded. *I won't bring him to Traveler for Astra to murder.*

Careful, SATIS said. *I could withdraw Astra and assign the mission to you. I know what he means to you. I understand compassion. See how I care for your sister in your absence?*

The image SATIS had beamed into her head might have been fake, but the threat was all too real. Viv, asleep in her bed on the Archipelago, curtains rustling as a stranger peered through the window. One of SATIS's assassins, watching.

Conor or Viv, SATIS had said. And LJ had made her choice.

"SATIS never knew I failed," LJ said. "That's what matters."

Viv sighed. "We'll have to find another way. There's got to be someone on the Archipelago who knows where to find Keyes's island."

But if there was, LJ had no idea how to go about finding them. With the shock dissipating, her head began to clear. "If we don't get there on Edward's heels, it'll be too late," she said. "We need them."

Viv studied her for a long time, as though scanning for wounds. LJ and the others might be programmed to kill, but Viv was programmed to help. Finally, she pushed off from the bar with a sigh. "OK. I'll convince them. But I think you'd better stay out of his way."

"He'd better stay out of mine," LJ called after her. But Viv was already pushing out the door, disappearing into the dusty din of the Plymouthport streets.

5

CONOR

Half an hour ago, Conor wouldn't have imagined that stepping into the streets of Plymouthport could be a relief under any circumstances. Even with the rancid smells and uncomfortable crowds coalescing around him, it felt better to be out in open air.

Away from her.

He'd have run, if he could. He gripped the head of the cane, grateful for its solidity.

"Dude," Trelawney said, "slow down. You're gonna open that wound."

It was already open. If not physically, then emotionally. Mentally. He felt undone, raw, like she was taking him apart from the inside out. He couldn't possibly get away from her fast enough.

Still, Conor slowed. He hadn't realized how fast he was hobbling. Frustration lanced through him, and he stepped over a milky puddle to pause on the side of the road. A hovercart bobbed by, and Trelawney scanned his wrist to purchase a bottle of water.

"Make sure the seal's not broken," Conor said.

Trelawney handed him the bottle, and Conor checked the seal before opening it himself. "You're not really walking away from this deal, are you?" Trelawney asked.

Conor gulped the water, his hands shaking so hard he nearly dropped it. "Find another ship."

Trelawney laughed. "Conor, man, there is no other ship. Not even people on Eding want to get anywhere near the guy who's shutting down the AIs. The council might've bought his spiel, but people are jumpy."

They'd definitely bought his spiel. That, or old Eddie had bought them. Conor grimaced at the thought; the old Conor would have given them more credit. The council was a committee that advised independent governments across the system, encompassing five entire planets and Marya's ever-changing network of livable moons. The council set regulations, but as to their real power... Conor wasn't sure how potent it really was.

Across the street, a pair of men spilled out of a tavern where the paint on the sign was so chipped that Conor couldn't make out the name. They were shouting at each other, stumbling around in the dirt. Punches were about to fly, but Conor doubted their mutual ability land a hit. No doubt they were seeing double.

"It won't matter how close they are," Conor said. "He's shutting down all the AIs on the planet to install his so-called patch."

"Yeah, you try explaining that." Trelawney tugged his ear, watching the fight develop across the street. One of the men yanked off his jacket and tossed it behind him. "It'll take days to find a ship. Your girl's ready to leave tomorrow."

"Not," Conor said. "Not my girl. She *stabbed* me, Parker. Stabbed."

"Only that one time," Trelawney said. "She could've killed you today, and she didn't."

"Not comforting."

Trelawney shrugged. "I'm a reporter. I deal in facts."

Conor glared at him. If anything, it seemed to him as though reporters dealt in sensation. Unfortunately, Parker wasn't wrong. Conor refused to care why Laura wanted to get to that island. She wouldn't find it without him, and that was all that mattered.

She looked different. That didn't matter, either, but he'd noticed, and it hammered at his chest along with everything else. She'd bleached the darkness out of her hair, and she wore her pistol openly at her hip. *Had* she changed? Or had she merely changed back to what she'd always been?

One of the fighters took a swing and stumbled face-forward in the dirt. Conor almost wished he'd made a wager on that. Was the sun always this hot here? He swigged the water, feeling woozy, his wound aching. He needed rest. He had no time.

The fallen fighter pulled himself to his knees just in time to get kicked in the face. Conor cringed as blood sprayed, curdling in the dirt.

"Look man, if you want to leave tomorrow, we need her ship," Trelawney said. "That's all there is."

"I don't trust her."

"You'd be a headcase, if you did. All the more reason to keep her close, yeah?"

Conor didn't want to keep her close. Every instinct told him to get as far from her as he could, to run until she'd never find him.

He didn't enjoy feeling like prey.

Across the street, the men stumbled into each other, knocked heads, and crumpled to the ground, groaning.

"That was anticlimactic," Trelawney said. He sounded disappointed.

Conor could see one of the women from the Spyglass heading toward them. The black woman who'd been watching from behind the bar, not the mouthy one. "How many of them are there?" he muttered. "Are they all...assassins?"

Trelawney clapped him on the shoulder. "Take heart, my man. Even if they are, they need you. You're basically their treasure map."

"So they're pirates," Conor said. "That's not better."

"You're the one who wanted to come to Eding," Trelawney said. "Come on, Keyes. Let's go get our ship."

Conor sighed. He cast a last glance back at the fighters, but they were stumbling away in opposite directions to sleep it off. Most places in the system, someone would have tried to separate them. Here, no one had even assembled to watch the brawl.

Conor really hated Eding. Stifling another sigh, he followed Trelawney through the crowd.

6

LJ

Fay's sleek, black yacht towered above the rest of the ships on the Plymouthport docks, as out of place among the rowboats and smuggling schooners as a skyscraper in a cornfield. Aside from its size, the ship's cleanliness made it sparkle in Toccata's early morning light, and it was clearly in perfect repair, while the surrounding vessels looked like a good kick might reduce them to a pile of floating boards.

So much for keeping the trip a secret. The way the other sailors—smugglers, pirates, whatever they called themselves—salivated as they watched the preparations, LJ expected a fight to break out any minute. Not that she'd have minded knocking a few heads together; after Conor's arrival yesterday, she could use some stress relief.

He was supposed to be dead, and he *wasn't* dead, and her relief was still so potent that she had to force herself to focus on her new mission, the one she couldn't fail. Resurrected lovers notwithstanding.

The shards of her past would be here waiting when she returned. She'd just have to sweep them up then.

As LJ and Viv made their way through the crowd, LJ couldn't help but check the pocket of her traveling coat for Conor's jammer. She'd withdrawn it from its hiding place in the floorboards of her room at the Spyglass, where she'd stashed the thing after stealing it from Conor as she fled the *Traveler*. It could be a useful thing to have.

No one had asked her about it, after she'd returned from the Star Leaders Academy. No one remembered it was why SATIS had wanted Conor dead. Not even Viv.

When LJ and Viv arrived at Fay's ship, the others were scurrying up and down the gangplanks, loading supplies while a crowd of onlookers gaped from the sidelines. For an AI who'd been so adept at subterfuge, SATIS had chosen an odd home for one of her assassins. Gilded portholes gleamed along the sides, offering glimpses of the luxurious cabins within the ship. The deck rose so high above the pier than the usual gangplank clearly wasn't an option; someone had patched together the world's most rickety ramp out of crates and boards. Still, the others seemed to be navigating it without trouble.

"Did Fay grow up on this boat?" LJ asked.

Viv shook her head, but she didn't elaborate. She never did.

A sailor from a neighboring boat reached out to touch the ship, and a curt male voice echoed from the yacht. "Unauthorized," it said. "Please step back."

LJ glanced at Viv in surprise. "Fay has another AI installed?"

"She replaced SATIS with a Nautical Onboard Assistant," Viv said. "NOA. Fay... Fay has trouble functioning free of SATIS."

"Don't we all," LJ muttered. Shouldering her duffel, she picked up a crate and followed Viv up the makeshift gangplank. Metallic gold paint on the bow named the ship *Robert Louis*. The decks were long and wide, as if primed for rows of lounge chairs, and as they reached the top, LJ noted a bamboo-roofed hut that looked suspiciously like a bar, though it had weapons strewn across it rather than drinks.

She didn't have much experience with tourism herself, but she thought the *Robert Louis* might have originally been designed as a cruise ship. She balanced her crate on the rail and watched as Sophie helped Bethany start up the maze of boards and crates toward the deck. Bethany's slow wobbling was causing a bottleneck; behind them, three more women waited patiently, arms laden with bags.

"Bethany should stay and keep an eye on the bar," LJ said.

"She didn't want to stay behind."

Of course, Viv would've already asked her. "We may need to pour out the booze, or she'll topple overboard the minute we hit a wave."

Viv didn't reply. LJ respected her sister's choice not to share the others' stories—she didn't want them gossiping about her, either—but she still didn't think letting Bethany drink to the point of drowning was the right call here. No matter what SATIS had done to her.

They were together now. They couldn't keep acting like a conference of islands.

Bethany stepped onto the deck, finally. When she caught them watching, she brushed imaginary dust off her shoulder and gave LJ a wink.

The rest of the ship made LJ think of a layered cake, one wrapped with ebony fondant and gold detailing along the edges. The open-air deck was wide, maybe as much as fifty yards across, with a checkerboard of vid screens across the bow that looked like a dance floor. The next layer of the ship-cake led to an enclosed corridor, presumably an entrance to the decks beneath their feet, with the pilot's deck stacked on top of that.

At least, LJ assumed it must be the pilot's deck, because Fay stood on the balcony outside the tinted windows, resting her arms on the rail and looking down at the preparations, her black hair drifting around her shoulders.

She looked innocent enough, but LJ had no intention of forgetting the look on Fay's face as she charged across the bar, hell-bent on murdering Viv.

Green Hair, who'd been stuck behind Bethany, broke free and dropped her crate beside the rail to join LJ and Viv, while LJ kept an eye on Fay. She half expected the woman to attack Viv again. Fay seemed to have changed her mind about that, but until LJ understood why, she wouldn't trust her.

Viv nudged LJ with an elbow, and she realized with a start that Green Hair had been speaking to her, not to Viv. "I'm sorry," LJ said. "What did you say?"

"I just wondered if everyone's here yet? I didn't see Tessa." Green Hair seemed to have forgotten yesterday's poker-game altercation; LJ was apparently still the boss.

"Um, I don't know," LJ said, trying to recall who Tessa was. Or who this woman was. It would be awkward to ask her now. Surely Viv knew the answer. "We just got here. She might be belowdecks?"

Green Hair nodded. "OK. If you see her, can you let her know I was looking for her? I have her bracelet."

LJ nodded absently, watching as Fay tapped something into her tab. Yes, she'd pivoted far too quickly from enemy to ally. She didn't have a business to save, or long-lost sisters to care for. What did she want out of this journey?

Viv nudged LJ again, and LJ realized that Green Hair was still waiting for a response. "Sure," she said, "will do."

The woman nodded uncertainly and walked away, hefting her crate back to her shoulders.

"Do you know her name?" Viv asked.

LJ looked reluctantly away from Fay to find her sister glaring at her. Viv rarely glared. "What's the matter?"

"She came to ask you a question. Do you know her name? Do you remember what she said?"

LJ did not know either of those things, and clearly Viv would not be the understanding source of information she'd hoped for. "Yes," she said, trying to cover. Not that she cared, really—not with a hundred other concerns battling for her attention—but Viv did. "That was Tessa, and she was looking for her bracelet."

Because maybe if she named *a* sister, Viv would go easy on her and assume LJ knew their names and had mixed them up. No big deal.

But Viv just shook her head and walked toward the gangplank to help with the crates.

"Vomit over the side if you feel sick, Bethany," Fay shouted from her perch. "NOA complains when I tell him to get out the swabbing bots, and I can't deal with his bitching right now. Ali, that crate goes belowdecks in the pantry. Sophie, Gretchen, NOA can direct you to storage."

Right. Green Hair, Gretchen. How the hell did Fay know everyone's names after only a handful of days?

The crowd on the dock jumbled, parting reluctantly to let Conor Keyes emerge from the pack. He used his cane for support as he stepped onto the makeshift gangplank, moving even slower than Bethany. His hair shone golden in the sunlight, his skin less pallid than it had been yesterday. Still, there were dark circles bruised beneath his eyes, and his lips were pressed tightly together. In pain, LJ thought. She'd done that.

She couldn't let guilt surface now just because Conor was alive. If anything, she should be absolved of it. But he looked thin, almost breakable, and that was her fault. LJ wanted to look away, but she couldn't make herself do it.

Parker Trelawney strode behind his friend in a palm-tree patterned shirt and neon green pants. Like he was boarding a pleasure cruise. He cast a wave to the crowd—which went ignored—but LJ could see that he was ready to leap in case Conor missed a step.

LJ had half a mind to go to Conor and offer him the jammer. A peace offering, but not an apology. It did belong to him, after all.

The other half of her wanted to throw it overboard, useful or not.

"I should go to the kitchen," LJ said, but she didn't move. She watched every step Conor made as he walked up the gangplank.

"Galley," Fay said, appearing at her side as if from nowhere. Ten seconds ago, she'd been up on that piratey balcony of hers. Unless LJ had been watching Conor for longer than she thought.

The idea was not a comfortable one. LJ shrugged, shaking off her unease and trying to look casual. "Ship or shore, a stove's a stove."

Conor made it onto the deck, and LJ breathed again. If there had been any other way to save the bar, and their sisters with it, she'd have done it. Anything to get away from the panic that crawled into her chest every time she laid eyes on him.

"You're thinking it's not too late to call this off," Fay said, "but it is. We're going."

Conor looked over and caught her watching him. He said something to Trelawney, who pointed the way belowdecks.

"I wasn't thinking that," LJ said.

Fay just smiled, like she knew the truth. She looked feral. It took a concerted effort not to flinch. "Please tell me you've got the balls to carry this out."

The activity on the deck slowed as the women who'd been ferrying crates past them caught the scent of their conversation and paused, their interest spreading across the ship. LJ watched Fay carefully, pretending not to notice the way everyone else—even Viv—had stopped to listen. "What do you mean?"

Fay's expression didn't change. "Will you really take the love code for yourself? For us?"

It was an effort to keep her posture relaxed, her hands unclenched. "Of course."

Fay leaned in closer, and LJ turned to face her. "Will you be able to kill him? If you have to?"

A few steps away, Viv tilted her head a fraction as if she, too, were interested in the answer. Everyone was, but LJ wondered what it meant that Viv could doubt her.

The women watched the conversation openly now, waiting for her response. Which was exactly what Fay wanted—though LJ still didn't know why. If there was a reason to cancel this little venture, it was her lack of faith in Fay's motives, and nothing else.

LJ swallowed. She breathed. And then, she lied. "Of course."

"Good," Fay said. "Then get ready, ladies. We're casting off."

7

CONOR

onor had grown up surrounded by opulent spaces. His father had a hover-train to traverse his mansion grounds on Verity, they were so enormous. He owned an office complex as big as a mid-sized Maryan city, and Conor's two-person family had frequently hopped from spaceport to spaceport in a ship built to carry fifty passengers. Even the Star Leaders Academy touring vessel, where Conor had gone to hide from his father, was ostentatiously beautiful, with its fancy bridges and greenery-decked stargazing parks.

The *Robert Louis* was among the more ridiculous modes of transport he'd stepped foot on. The black siding beamed like a polished stone, reflecting Toccata's light in blinding shards, and its height felt absolutely unnecessary.

This ship might have been stripped of everything that made it a luxury vessel—aside from the ridiculous dance floor, and a rogue strand of lights on the nav deck balcony, crowning the crew of heavily armed assassins with grotesque cheer—but there was no doubt the *Robert Louis* had been designed for opulence. The tinted windows on the nav deck made it resemble a limousine, or like it was wearing sunglasses like the ones Laura had had perched on her face up on deck.

Just the thought of Laura made him grip the handle of his cane harder as he navigated his way belowdecks, Trelawney still hovering at his side. Conor couldn't believe he'd agreed to get on a ship with her. To come within a mile of her, even.

And yet, here he was. Conor's stomach turned with unease, but more than that, it was unexpressed frustration. It was that no matter how he lectured himself, he could not convince his heart to be afraid of her now that the initial shock of seeing her had passed.

Angry, yes. Bitter, resentful. But afraid? He searched his feelings, and he came up short. And that felt more dangerous than anything. His brain blasted warnings at him, leaving his heart in a tangle of confusion.

The ship's interior smelled like dried flowers and salt-water sea. The entry hall was clean and carpeted as if it were a resort hotel, and Conor wondered where these women could have procured such a ship. Stolen, no doubt.

At least there were no tiny ladders or spiral staircases. Conor took the elevator, dismissing Trelawney to locate his own accommodations. Parker meant well, but if the man didn't stop hovering at Conor's elbow as if his wound might split open at any moment, they were going to have words. Yes, the trek up that teetering pile of boards had made life touch-and-go for a few harrowing moments, but he'd made it. No problem.

When he reached the row of passenger cabins, Conor entered the first open door and shut it behind him. The ship might be big enough for bowling alleys and ballrooms, but the cabin was compact. It smelled new, like a freshly opened pack of cables. Like no one had ever set foot inside.

Conor sat on the narrow bed and considered the space. Luxury in a ship's cabin like this one was all in the details. Passengers wouldn't be expected to remain in their rooms, but to stroll the upper decks, gamble in the bar, dance in the ballroom. Here, the lighting fixtures were simple but expensive, the glass delicately fluted around the bulbs. The handles on the drawers were shaped into elegant swirls. The top of the bureau boasted a hot plate and a coffee pod installed in the wall.

Simple, boring elegance. Conor stood, grunting as the wound pulled. He opened a cabinet and peered inside, looking for a refrigerator.

"May I assist you in locating any amenities?"

Conor jumped as the voice echoed into his room, a smooth baritone that called to mind butlers in historical vids. Someone with shiny buttons and starched collars.

Trelawney had warned him that the ship had an AI.

"No," Conor said curtly. "I'd thank you to leave my room entirely."

He regretted the loss of his jammer. He hadn't found it among his things in *Traveler*'s med bay, which could mean it was still in his cabin on the Star Leaders vessel. Or that Laura had taken it. With the jammer, he could control the AI's access to his room, or widen the scope to hamper its abilities across the whole ship. He'd been meaning to make another one, but he hadn't yet had the chance. Time was ever against him.

He'd been settling in to make a prototype for Astra that night, before Laura had betrayed him. What had become of

Astra, without his assistance? Her AI was gone, or so Laura and her band of killers claimed. Had Astra escaped? Or was she another casualty to his father's madness?

"Apologies," the *Robert Louis* AI said. "I will not trouble you again."

Conor opened another cabinet, the drawer under the bed, and a narrow closet that contained two empty hangers and a miniature safe. He'd expected to find a refrigerator somewhere in the room—his medication needed to be chilled, and soon—but there was nothing.

"Um," he said. "AI?"

"Yes?"

Even though he needed the computer's help, the voice sent annoyance surging through Conor's chest. He imagined he could feel the computer's presence, like a humming in his bones, like a phantom at his back that vanished when he turned. Always out of eyesight. "I thought you were going to leave me alone."

"Of course, sir. By maintaining my silence."

"I meant I wanted you out of the cameras. Out of the room."

"But how would I assist with your inquiries?"

Conor ground his teeth. "I would like you to vacate my cabin entirely."

"As you like, sir." A beat of silence. "Were you searching for something?"

Conor closed his eyes, then immediately regretted it. The situation might force him into proximity with an AI, but if he controlled his physical reactions, the computer wouldn't be able to read him as clearly.

But then, he *had* been searching for something. Conor sighed. The AI was probably a basic vessel model, less powerful than *Traveler*'s SPA and designed to assist passengers. It would not fall in love, or try to take over the system, or decide it could best assist them by blowing their ship out of the water. Probably.

He could ask for something simple, just this once. "I have medication I need chilled. Is there a refrigeration unit in the room?"

"I'm afraid not, sir," the AI responded. "You'll have to go to the galley for that. Next level down, at the end of the hall."

Conor stood and pulled his cooler pack of healing expeditors out of his bag. Might as well deliver it to the fridge now. It would be unfortunate if they went bad. He'd still be fine, with all the antibiotics and such pulsing through his body, but he'd be patched up and on his feet much faster with the meds to help his cells.

"Will that be all, sir?" the AI said.

"You really can't take a hint, can you?"

"No, sir. I was designed to obey direct orders."

"Then stay out of this room. Whatever your name is."

"Nautical Operations Assistant. NOA."

Great. Someone had gotten cute with their acronyms. Conor squashed a joke about assassins arriving two by two, alongside the sheep and the goats. Humor might encourage the machine to keep talking to him.

"OK. NOA. Stay out of the cameras. Stay out of the mics. Stay out of the speakers."

"I am unable to override general ship announcements."

Conor's jaw creaked and he forced his teeth apart. "Just —bare minimum. All right? If I call you from here and you respond, I'll dismantle you piece by bloody piece."

The AI didn't respond. Finally.

Someone else who'd been raised by the system's foremost expert on AI tech might have been as obsessed with the nosy computers as the rest of the world. Might have cashed in, even. Might have welcomed his legacy.

But Conor knew how easily AIs could be manipulated, and how quickly his father was willing to do it. Dad would create a Toccata System Empire by spreading the base of the code that had left SATIS devoted to him, and with every AI in Toccata leaping to do his bidding, he'd control everything. Governments. Mining operations. Ship navigation, household necessities, and bank accounts. *Every* bank account.

Besides, other people could have nefarious plans, too. Dad certainly wasn't the only knowledgeable AI scientist in the system. If Conor got his way, NOA—and every other AI in the system—would soon be extinct.

Conor stepped out into the hall. He half expected NOA to chime back into the speakers with another request to assist him, but the computer kept its thoughts—if it had any —to itself. Still, Conor could feel the thing's eyes on him as he moved through the passage. He shivered, imagining what the AI might be researching about him right now. What details it might be cataloguing for later use.

A good number of the doors along the passageway were still open, revealing empty cabins as compact as his own. Everyone else seemed to be above, though. Just as well. He didn't care to run into any assassins.

Conor took the stairs down, using his cane for balance, and followed NOA's directions toward the galley. He barely needed instructions; the whole passage smelled like sautéing garlic. He followed his nose to the end of the hall, stopping short in the doorway when he saw who was responsible for it.

Laura. He should have realized. She was kneading a lump of dough, her arms dusted to the elbows with flour.

Her hair grazed her shoulders in messy, bleached waves, her tank top showing off the cuff of black knots she had tattooed on her right bicep. She'd told him once they were a throwback to an Earthen culture, one from which she supposedly descended. He'd traced them with his fingertip. He knew about the other, a trio of interconnected teardrops on her hip.

"What do you want?" Laura said, though she hadn't looked up.

Conor swallowed and held up the cooler, forcing himself to remember the look in her eyes as she'd plunged the knife into his gut. That should not be something he needed to remind himself of. "I need to chill these."

She kept her eyes on the dough, as though it commanded her full attention. "Then tie them to a rope and drag them behind the ship. I'm not an infirmary."

Infirmary. He hadn't thought to ask about that. "The galley's close to my cabin," he said, though he had no idea where the infirmary was, or why he wouldn't accept any excuse to get away from her.

Laura brushed a lock of hair out of her face with the back of her hand, leaving a smudge of flour across her forehead, then rolled her eyes. "Fine, leave it. I'll put it in the fridge."

Conor laughed, doing everything he could to make it sound derisive. "Excuse me if I don't trust you to handle one of the medications that's currently keeping me alive."

"So you're going to pop it into the fridge and leave it in the room with me, trusting that I won't simply wait until you leave to slip in a drop of poison? But stars forbid I should transport the thing with my own hands from the counter to the fridge. You might perish terribly."

There was no passion in her tone, no anger. Just pure,

sardonic disdain. He'd seen it leveled at plenty of people, including Astra when they'd first met—Laura must have known, then, who she was—but the full blast of the mocking tone still hit him in the chest. As if he'd been the one to hurt her.

"I could kill you right now with my bare hands," she continued. "Or a kitchen knife, or the Edinburgh I've got strapped to my hip. You're already trusting me."

An old quote about protestations and truthfulness floated into his mind, a passage his Laura would have appreciated. Conor tossed it aside, watching her as she pummeled the wad of dough.

Laura might be the greatest actress in the system, but the problem was he didn't know *which* Laura was the act. Was it this angry woman who seemed determined to punch him with her disdain? Or was it the woman he'd asked to marry him only a few weeks ago? It wasn't as if they'd spent a bare few weeks together; it had been an entire year. Conor hadn't felt right continuing to employ her once they were together, but she'd refused to leave her guard position, and it would have been even more wrong to fire her. So they kept on, hip to hip, days blurring into nights blurring into mornings.

She knew everything about him. What had happened with SimuBot, and all of Conor's secrets. All but the most shameful one.

But Conor knew her tells, too. Laura cooked all the time, like a compulsion. It had felt incongruous after he'd first watched her spar, taking down five of his best guards in a bare-knuckled frenzy. As if a woman couldn't be capable of both violence and ingenuity in the kitchen.

Yes, Laura cooked all the time. But she baked when she felt lost. A talk with her sister, a furtive call on her com, and they'd be eating fresh bread for days.

Oh, it could have been a farce, but he didn't think so. Now, he was watching her punish the dough as if it had personally offended her, and he couldn't forget how often he'd woken early to find her out of his bed and hiding in the kitchen. On his ship. In his apartment on Verity. Even during that too-short vacation they'd taken on Quin. Punching dough, just like she was now.

"You keep saying you can kill me," Conor said carefully, "but I have trouble believing you."

She raised her eyebrows, darting a glance to his gut. It took everything he had not to cover his wound in protection. She couldn't hurt him with a look. And he couldn't forgive her, but that didn't mean he was still afraid.

But that was the entire problem, wasn't it? He should be afraid. He should be running, not thinking about who was real and who wasn't.

Maintaining his grip on the bag, and his cane, Conor stepped forward and leaned over the counter, the smell of yeast and olive oil assaulting his senses with memory. He would ask her, and when she refused to answer he would ask again, and he would keep asking—why, why, why had she done it?—until she gave him a damn answer.

He opened his mouth, but Laura anticipated his question, speaking before he could. "I was following orders."

Apparently she knew his tells, too. It was comforting, in a way, that she at least remembered. "To kill me," he said.

She shrugged.

"And the rest of it?"

He hated himself, a little bit, for asking. As if his pride were so wounded by her betrayal that he needed to hear some of what existed between them had been true. What did he want her to say? That she'd loved him and stabbed him anyway?

Right. Because that would make it better.

Laura snatched the bag off the counter and whirled around, leaving smears of flour on the top as she stuffed it into the refrigerator. "There. Your meds are cold. You won't die today. Now get out of my kitchen."

8

LJ

Cooking for a crew of thirty wasn't the same thing as hiding. Yes, LJ had brought enough food to feed them all for three voyages, but what if she'd miscalculated? Music thumped from the upper deck, where someone must have figured out how to activate the sound system that accompanied the vid-screen dance floor she'd noticed when they first arrived. LJ had absolutely no interest in joining the party.

She'd managed to keep everyone happily fed on fish, soup, and bread for the past two days, and all without engaging in more than a cursory conversation. LJ didn't count the barbs she'd exchanged with Conor in here over his medication as the *Robert Louis* set sail. Even Viv seemed to be avoiding her.

LJ dusted the stainless-steel counter with flour, missing her kitchen back at the Spyglass. The tavern had chop marks in the countertops and dim lighting, but she never bumped her head on the stove hood and there was plenty of room for leaving mounds of dough to rise. And, important detail, no one's anti-death medications stared her down whenever she opened the refrigerator.

"If you bake any more bread, we're going to have to sacrifice it to the gulls."

Viv was leaning in the doorway, her beret tipped at an angle. LJ didn't know when she'd arrived, or how long she'd been watching. Viv was good at sneaking up on people. She had to be; she'd managed baby assassins for half her life.

"Everyone's up on deck," Viv said. "It's kind of a party."

"So you're saying I should have made cookies?"

"With sprinkles."

It was like this whole voyage was a bonding exercise for Viv, a chance to push everyone together and force them to be friends. Like this was nothing more than a high-stakes scavenger hunt. LJ plunged her hands into the dough and flipped the sticky mess over with a wet smack. "I can't imagine this many actual sisters getting along, let alone... whatever we are. Some of us will always hate each other."

Like Fay. The others might have accepted her because she'd offered them a boat, but LJ hadn't. The feeling, she could tell, was entirely mutual.

Viv tugged at her hoop earring. "You'll be friends with no one if you stay down here."

"I'm friends with you."

"Lucky me. Come on. You could use some fresh air. They're not so bad."

LJ sighed. It wasn't the sisters she was concerned about, not really, but she couldn't bring herself to ask if Conor was abovedecks, too. What did it matter? She'd put in an appearance, walk the circuit, and disappear as soon as Viv was preoccupied with someone else.

LJ couldn't bring herself to disappoint her sister. Not when Viv stood there with that practiced nonchalance, doing her best to hide the hope in her eyes. She always wanted to save everyone, and apparently that included LJ.

Sighing, LJ gave the dough a final punch, then brushed off her hands on a towel. "Lead the way."

Eding had no moon, but the yacht's lights seemed designed to imitate the silvery glow that lit the heavens on other planets. LJ half wanted to ask NOA to switch them off so she could see the river of stars that chased them from above; even with the lights on, starlight glanced through the waves like skipping rocks, giving the impression that they were sailing through an infinite, glowing dandelion.

LJ frowned, pulling her gaze from the sky and tamping down the feeling of wonder that came along with it. She didn't like wonder. It made her feel small.

The music was significantly louder on deck, bass vibrating through the now-flashing floorboard screens to accompany frequent peals of laughter that the over-whelming smell of rum explained perfectly. "We're announcing ourselves to the entire planet here," LJ said, watching as Bethany whirled another girl across the dance floor. LJ really needed to learn more of their names.

Viv scoffed. "What does that matter? That one already told the whole system we're going." Viv tugged a thumb toward the bow, where Parker Trelawney sat wearing a bowler that was dusted with rhinestones, of all things. He wasn't exactly discrete.

LJ's gaze skipped past him to land on Conor. He hadn't seen her yet; the two men sat together, heads bent over some project—Conor was always working on some project— gears and chips spread before them on a blanket.

For a woman raised by a computer, LJ didn't have much of a mind for technology. Still, she'd spent hours at Conor's side while he sorted through projects like the one he worked on now. She hadn't been able to help much, but she'd asked questions. And guarded the door.

No doubt Trelawney made a better partner. She'd been aware of their friendship, if vaguely. Conor had maintained a revolving supply of surface-level friendships, and though she'd never met his reporter friend, LJ had assumed when Conor talked about the war correspondent that their relationship fell into the same category. Trelawney was a disaster when it came to stealth, but he seemed to have steady hands, and a lot more to say about Conor's work than LJ ever had. There wasn't any reason for the indignant flush that pulsed across her skin, but the sight of him in the place she'd occupied for so long made her throat contract with jealousy.

"What are they doing?" LJ asked, working to keep her voice level.

"He says he has to make something to get us access to the island," Viv said. "He didn't tell me what."

"I thought he knew exactly where we were going."

Maybe he'd withheld the coordinates, though. She could see him doing something like that. It was a good thing she'd kept the jammer from him—who knew what trouble they'd be dealing with if he decided to shut down NOA—though she wouldn't put it past him to rebuild it.

"You gonna go ask him to clarify?" Viv said.

"Nope."

"Didn't think so." Viv stood there next to her, and LJ could practically hear the unasked question. Her sister was waiting for an explanation, for LJ to grab a pint of ice cream and tell her what had happened during that year she'd spent working as his guard.

Viv was a smart woman. She'd figure it out. When LJ didn't reply, her sister crossed the deck and crouched beside

Trelawney. LJ half expected the men to chase her off, but they didn't.

Feeling lost, LJ wandered over to a circle of women sitting nearby, a blanket spread beneath them. When LJ joined them, their conversation tapered, though Sophie patted her knee in welcome. Bethany still danced with the same woman on the deck, though now they were trying some kind of weird step where they kept their hands propped on their hips and clacked their feet around like goats. They were laughing.

Maybe some of them could be friends. Maybe.

"What are we talking about?" LJ said. "Dolls? Ribbons? Landry City's weird new veil fetish?"

"SATIS," Fay said. She lounged against the side of the boat, arms propped up along the bench, legs spread out in front of her. She had her head tipped back to stare at the stars, but LJ had the sense that she was paying attention to everything on deck. The conversation, the dancers, the men scheming at the bow.

"Oh, SATIS. Nifty," LJ said. "The kidnapping? The twenty-four hour surveillance? Or was it the part where she trained us all to murder anyone who disagreed with her?"

"That part bugging you, Elj?" Fay said, her eyes darting briefly to the men at the bow. "Feeling guilty?"

"Not at all. It's just, I got addicted to killing and now there's no one to give me missions. It's a shame."

"She rescued me," Sophie said softly, and LJ wrenched her gaze away from Fay to look at her. She was petite for one of SATIS's assassins, not that the AI could have predicted any of their sizes when she'd taken them in. Then again, maybe she could. LJ wouldn't have put it past her.

But Sophie barely cleared five feet. The cloud of white-blond hair that puffed around her face gave her a vulnerable look. Like she didn't belong. Still, the muscles in her upper arms were well defined. She'd definitely trained.

Fay looked up, and the other women in the circle stilled, too. Bethany kept dancing on the deck; Parker Trelawney left his place at Conor's side, dragging Viv over to join him. Viv dancing. When had LJ ever seen Viv dance?

"I remember it," Sophie said. "I was... My family lived on Orthos, back in the monarchy days. The king decided my father had..." She swallowed, gave her head a little shake. "We were just farmers. Daddy filled orders—he didn't ask about politics. And one day he filled a large one."

"He fed the rebellion," Fay said.

Sophie nodded. The rest of the women were still watching her, Fay included, but while the others looked sympathetic, Fay clenched her fists in her lap. A muscle in her jaw twitched as she clamped her teeth together.

Fay was angry, but not because Sophie had been hurt. How was it that no one else saw that?

Sophie drew circles on the deck with her finger, trailing a bead of water around the ebony plasteel. "The king's men killed my mother in front of him. Then they killed him. I lived on the street for three years. By the time the rebels took over, I was almost starved."

LJ glanced in Viv's direction, hoping for confirmation of the story before realizing that her sister hadn't heard. She was still dancing.

LJ didn't think Sophie would lie, anyway. And something about the way Fay was staring at the younger girl made LJ believe the story even more. Who had Fay been, before SATIS?

Gretchen put a hand on Sophie's arm. "And SATIS saved you."

"I have no idea how she got to Orthos in the first place,"

Sophie said. Neither did LJ. SATIS had needed physical assistance to spread away from her stations, and the timing would have predated Viv's role as the AI's hands. "I just know she saved my life. I miss her."

Silence. LJ glanced at the other women, trying to discern their feelings. Cuff—she must be Tessa, now that LJ considered it—was focused on Sophie, sympathy burning in her dark eyes. The others just stared at the deck, lost in their own memories.

And Fay considered them all, like a wolf running inventory on a chicken coop.

"What about you, Fay?" LJ said. "Where are you from?"

The others shifted slightly, fidgeting hands and shifting weight flurrying at the edges of her awareness. It wasn't a question they asked. It was information they volunteered. But LJ kept her attention on Fay, hoping for a reaction. Reading people wasn't her specialty—that was Viv's arena, and Astra's—but LJ knew how to pay attention.

Fay locked eyes with her and smiled. "It's all up to you, isn't it, boss?" she said. "You'll get us to SATIS."

LJ blinked. "SATIS's resources, you mean."

"Of course," Fay said. "Her resources."

The look on Fay's face told her it hadn't been a slip, but LJ couldn't say what it meant. Whatever game Fay was playing, the other woman seemed to think she was winning. And that was disconcerting.

A tear slipped down Sophie's cheek, and LJ got to her feet. That was more than enough bonding for one night. For a lifetime, really, though LJ doubted Viv would let her off so easily.

As she straightened, she looked back over the deck for a last glance at the stars. Instead, she found herself meeting Conor's gaze, cutting across the darkness like an icy blade.

From here, his eyes were just pools in the darkness. She imagined the stars reflected in them, like little pinpoints of pain.

His expression didn't change. He just stared at her, unmoving, until she turned away to stalk toward the stairs with her heart pulsing in her throat.

She was halfway there when NOA's voice piped over the speaker system, grainy and interspersed with crackles.

"Pardon the interruption," NOA said, his gentleman's accent splitting the silence with polite urgency, as if he meant to ask for directions, "but I believe we're about to be attacked."

9

CONOR

Trelawney materialized at Conor's side while NOA was still spitting out stats about ETA and guessing at the number of armed attackers on the approaching ship. Already, the assassins were preparing to fight. They scuttled up the masts and ducked behind rails, knives and guns slipping out of sleeves and shoes like it was nothing out of the ordinary.

They could fight. He'd seen that firsthand. But they were assassins, not soldiers. They didn't know how to coordinate on a battlefield, and that was going to be a problem. One he couldn't fix.

Conor set his hands on the rail and looked out across the water. No moon, no warning, if not for the AI. But their enemies, whoever they were, had likely used another one to find them in the first place, so round and round the problem circled. That one he *would* fix. If they survived.

The other ship had turned its lights off, but when he relaxed his eyes, he could make out its rippling wake as it roared toward them across the waves.

"We should go dark," he said.

"Agreed," NOA responded, and the lights blinked off.

Conor ground his teeth. "I didn't mean you."

"I've scanned local vessels," NOA said, as though Conor hadn't spoken. "The make and size of this one matches a schooner that was docked beside us when we departed. Though I think it may have been stolen."

The AI managed to sound vaguely scandalized by the prospect.

Laura joined Conor at the rail, along with Viv and the angry one who owned the boat. Ship. They were no more than silhouettes, Laura's hair tied back in a messy braid. She smelled like rosemary. "They followed us," she said. "I'm actually a little impressed."

"At their ingenuity?" Conor asked.

"At their follow through."

The angry one spat over the rail. "They have cannons?"

"No, but my scan shows the figures on the schooner are outfitted in mechanized armor," NOA said. "They will be within shooting range in approximately four minutes."

"No way," Bethany called, half staggering toward them from her hiding place in the bow where Conor and Trelawney had been working. Her words slurred together; she'd clearly been drinking as much as she'd been dancing. "Robo pirates? I want one. Can we keep one?"

Conor found it difficult to believe that Bethany had ever been an assassin.

Laura turned to face her. Behind her, Viv looked concerned, though he couldn't tell if she was more worried about Bethany or Laura.

"Go belowdecks," Laura said. "We'll check on you after we sink them."

Viv cringed.

"Nah," Bethany said, twirling a blade between her

fingers. For all her staggering around, she did manage not to cut herself. "Staying."

For a beat, Laura remained perfectly still. And then she lunged, moving so fast that Conor flinched. But she blurred straight past him, and when she stopped, she had Bethany by the upper arm, her pistol in her hand, though she kept the barrel pointed at the deck. "If I were a pirate, you'd be dead right now," she said.

"I can fight."

Laura shoved her away, and Bethany tripped, catching herself with a hand as she fell. She winced, cradling her wrist in front of her.

"Get below," Laura said. "Now."

Bethany stood, stumbled, and steadied herself before walking slowly toward the door and for some reason, Viv shook her head at Laura. Conor wasn't sure Laura saw the look her sister gave her, or maybe she was ignoring it; Laura had spoken of Viv, and often, though she'd brushed off any suggestion of his meeting her. While he grasped the reason for that now, he clearly didn't understand the dynamics between them.

Still, he wasn't sure Bethany should be up here, either. She might hurt herself, or shoot one of her sisters by accident. He almost opened his mouth to defend Laura's decision before he realized what he was doing, and bit the inside of his cheek instead, holding back the traitorous words. Habits. They died hard.

"We need to arm NOA," Fay said. "His cannons can blow them out of the water before they're in range."

"No," Conor said.

All three silhouettes turned to look at him, and Trelawney besides. Conor swallowed, scrambling for an explanation, for anything he could say to keep them from giving the AI a chance to shoot things.

"They'll turn our AI against us," he said finally.

It was weak, and he knew it. But he didn't retract it.

"I am not easily corruptible," NOA said. "And I have a name."

"The more personality they have," Conor said pointedly, "the more easily corruptible they are."

Fay turned to Laura. Conor wasn't sure which of them was in charge here; he sensed a push and pull, but Fay seemed to be appealing to Laura for a decision. "We have to be able to shoot at them," she said.

"Three minutes," NOA said.

The schooner was close enough to be heard now, water sluicing along its sides to the tune of metallic clicks and clanks as its crew prepared to blast them off the decks.

Conor stepped around Fay. "Lor," he said, "trust me on this. We cannot arm that AI."

"I only wish to assist," NOA said.

"Shut up," Conor and Laura said together. She frowned at him, like she hoped to oust any hint of a lie just by staring at him. The irony of it made him want to burst out laughing.

"Two minutes," NOA said.

The other ship switched on its lights, blinding rays piercing through the blackness as the pirates opened fire from the deck. For a few seconds, Conor could see nothing but white. But NOA's calculations were correct; they were still out of range.

When his vision returned, he almost wished they'd kept the lights off. Armored men and women lined the deck of the schooner, their metal suits no less intimidating for consisting of mish-mashing colors, ill-fitted hacks, and streaks of rust. Their boots made them giants, helmets towering high above the decks.

"I'll be damned," Laura said. "They really are robo pirates."

In spite of himself, Conor laughed.

"One minute," NOA said.

Conor took a deep breath and cupped his hands along the side of his mouth. "You might not want to kill us just yet," he said. "I'd make an excellent hostage."

Laura wrapped her fingers around his arm, pulling him a step back from the rail. Her touch burned. "You can't possibly think your father would pay a ransom for you. He wanted you killed."

"Good thing someone else got there first," he bit back. She drew her hand away as if stung, but she wasn't wrong. In fact, when Astra had first admitted she'd come to the *Traveler* to kill him, Conor had assumed it was his father who'd sent her.

He shouldn't believe in Edward Keyes's redemption. But the man who laughed at Conor's mistrust of AIs was indistinguishable from the father who'd ushered him around the system throughout his childhood, personally educating him, patiently answering his questions. Loving him, for all the good that did.

Even if Conor could give his father's soul up for lost, he knew what no one else did: that he needed redemption as badly as Edward Keyes ever had. If he didn't offer that chance to his father, why should he deserve one himself?

The pirates were arguing on the deck, shaking armored arms at each other as they debated—he hoped—the benefits of a lucrative hostage. Maybe that would make them hesitate to kill everyone before taking the ship.

Laura had one hand on her pocket, an idea threaded in the crease between her eyebrows. "NOA," she said, "is their armor AI operated?"

"Yes," NOA said. "It's run by an ARMPIT model. Unfortunate acronym, isn't it, though someone worked hard to get it there. It stands for ARMor aPtitude Informa—"

A shot blasted from the *Robert Louis*'s rigging, cutting off the rest of NOA's speech. The bullet clinked against one of the pirates' suits, causing him to take a single step backward.

"Run," Conor said. "NOA, we need to run."

The *Robert Louis* sprang to life so quickly that Conor nearly fell, the wound in his gut stabbing him anew. Laura reached out to steady him, but it was all he could do not to double over in pain. Where had he left his cane?

"We can't outrun them," Fay said.

As if in answer, one of the pirates propped a gun against the rail, its barrel the size of a drainage pipe. Conor had only a moment to shout a warning before a deep boom echoed across the water, a line of smoke snaking over the waves toward the *Robert Louis*'s hull.

10

LJ

The ship lurched, knocking LJ off her feet and pushing her into a slide across the deck. She slammed into the opposite rail a split second before Fay landed beside her, head spinning as the sky churned dizzily above. A figure toppled from the rigging, screaming as she bloodied her hands catching herself on one of the hanging ropes. The girl who'd shot at the pirates, if LJ had to make a guess.

The yacht plunged back down, the bow diving into the waves before resurfacing with a violent roll. The handful of women who'd stationed themselves at the front of the ship emerged from the deluge, gasping for air as they ran for the perceived safety of the center.

LJ wasn't sure there was safety in the center. Or anywhere.

"NOA, activate the sweeps and patch that leak," Fay said, her words right in LJ's ear.

LJ scrambled up as water sloshed over the side of the ship, coating the insides of her nostrils in burning saltwater. The deck vibrated beneath her feet as cannons unfurled from the side of the ship. SATIS had just loved to modify perfectly innocent vehicles to make them deadly.

LJ scanned the deck, staggering as the ship listed forward and back up again. Viv was helping one woman to her feet, while Sophie staggered around checking on the others. It was Tessa who'd caught the rope above, and she hit the deck with freely bleeding hands.

LJ didn't mean to look for Conor, and she definitely didn't mean to let out a breath of relief when her eyes finally found him braced along the opposite rail, half curled over his wound and staring back toward the ship that had just fired on them, with Trelawney hovering over him like a worried hen.

"Put the guns away," Conor shouted, "reel them back in. Laura, you can't let the AI keep control."

"I am perfectly trustworthy," NOA protested which, unfortunately, made him sound the opposite.

Conor hauled himself to his feet and staggered toward her, water streaming down his face.

LJ dug into her pocket, fingers closing around the edges of the jammer. If she gave it to him, there'd be no turning back.

In the background, the pirates on the other ship were shouting. Their ragtag armor hid some of their faces, but several hadn't bothered to close their visors. One of them, a man with a lined slab of a face that made LJ think of melted rock, sprinted across the deck of the schooner, using the suit to vault him over the rail and across the short gap to the *Robert Louis*. Ragtag armor or not, it was perfectly capable of swinging him up onto the deck.

LJ let go of the jammer and drew the Edinburgh instead, rushing across the deck to bring her within a decent range. Tessa was closer, and she charged, wielding a pole like a quarterstaff in her bloodied hands as one of the other assassins ran in from the opposite side.

Tessa landed a blow to the pirate's back before he batted them both away, knocking them to the ground. LJ reached them and fired, her shot glancing off the armor like a pin. The pirate lifted a fist in her direction, the chaos on the deck reflected as a tinted contortion in the glass of his visor, and LJ dove behind a storage crate before he could shoot at her with whatever firepower he had installed in those forearms.

"Cannons at the ready," NOA said, his voice cutting across the noise.

NOA could shoot at the other ship all he wanted, but one robo pirate in an armored suit could take them all down. That ship had a dozen, at least. LJ pulled the jammer out of her pocket and crawled back across the deck to Conor, still crouched where she'd left him on the port side railing. The pirate's hulking steps rang through the frenzy, punctuated by frantic gunshots as the others raced to attack him.

LJ landed next to Conor, avoiding his eyes as she shoved the jammer into his hand, the weight of their history passing between them with that one gesture. In a way, this whole mess hinged around that tiny silver box.

Conor slipped the box open and compressed the button on the device inside it, activating the AI jammer. NOA's voice fell silent, and the robo pirate froze near the starboard rail, his right arm half raised.

Across the deck, Fay issued a stream of curses and dove toward the ladder to the pilot's deck, shouting for someone named Ali to repair the hull while she took manual control of the ship. As they ran, two of the assassins vaulted out of their hiding places to tip the pirate over the rail, armor and all.

On the other ship, chaos reigned as the pirates tried to escape their frozen shells. Their ship bobbed, aimless, as Fay took control and the *Robert Louis* sped away.

Conor swayed beside LJ, bracing himself on the rail and staring at the box like it could take him back in time.

"You're welcome," she said.

Conor blinked and looked up, as if he'd forgotten she was there. He slipped the jammer into his pocket. "I'm not going to thank you for giving me what's mine."

Fay reappeared on the pilot's deck, her face a mask of rage as she swung down.

"Shouldn't you be driving?" LJ said. Not that she expected the other woman to leave that easily, but a girl could hope.

"The ship probably has autopilot," Conor said. "Pro-grammed navigation, rather than AI assisted."

Like his spaceship, she remembered, and the pods that carried him from ship to planet.

Fay stalked across the deck, and LJ tensed, expecting an attack. But Fay drew up short, jabbing a finger in Conor's direction. "He could have gotten us killed."

"He didn't, though," Viv said. "He killed their suits."

Fay spat blood over the rail. "And our AI. We're hobbled. Without NOA, Keyes will be in and out before we're halfway to the island."

"I can get the pumps working and fix the hull," Conor said. "We don't need an AI for that."

"Or you could reactivate NOA and let him fix it," Fay said.

Conor just shook his head. LJ knew what his father had done, how Keyes had twisted Conor's AI invention and exploited lives for the sake of profit. Conor's fear ran deeper than a hobbled ship, especially if he thought he could repair it himself.

Fay raised a finger and pointed it in LJ's face. "You promised you'd do what needs to be done."

"I will," LJ said, batting the woman's hand away. She tried to twist Fay's wrist, to gain the upper hand, but Fay sidestepped, knocking LJ off balance. SATIS couldn't have bothered to teach them different fighting techniques, could she? All that knowledge, distilled into one assassin-producing machine.

"We can't find the island without Conor, or navigate it once we get there," LJ said.

"I don't trust you," Fay said to Conor, who was still standing there looking... eerily focused. "You're his son. You know what he did to her."

All at once, LJ noticed the way the rest of the assassins were watching Conor, eyes touched with anger, fear, and betrayal. Even Sophie looked ready to attack. Had they been looking at him that way all along? They'd all been raised to hate his father. They'd been raised to hate *him*. How had she not have seen the danger?

"I'll get us to the island," Conor said.

Fay shook her head and spat again. "Get my AI back online," she said. With that, she turned on her heel and marched back to the pilot's deck.

Conor stayed where he was, one hand on the pocket where he'd stashed the jammer. "What did she mean?" he said. "What needs to be done?"

LJ just shook her head. What was she supposed to say? That Fay wanted her to kill him? That she couldn't do it?

Unable to form an answer, and hating herself for it, she turned away.

LJ's LEGS were jittering after the roller coaster ride on the deck, her heart refusing to slow. She tried to breathe, but it felt like someone had wrapped a vice around her chest.

Thankfully, the jammer didn't affect the elevator. Conor had managed a working AI jammer long before he'd met LJ, but it hadn't been until she'd entered his employ that he'd figured out how to keep essential functions like elevators running. Or, on a spaceship, artificial gravity and life support. As he explained it, the jammer forced the AI to continue those aspects the same way the human body breathed; while the computer slept, the functions ticked on.

To Conor, it had been a major accomplishment.

LJ knew she should probably go see if she could help with the hull repair instead of running away, but she couldn't face him for another second. So instead, she made her way to the ballroom. Because the ballroom had a bar.

They'd been eating up on deck for the most part, the ballroom too stuffy and overdecorated for anyone's comfort. Gilded mirrors were set along the walls in an effort to make the space seem larger, the plush velvet carpet sinking a full inch as she crossed the room. LJ had come in a few times—there was a pantry hatch in the floor behind the bar, good for storing extra bread—but she hadn't lingered.

It was the kind of place SATIS had loved.

Bethany sat at the end of the bar like she always did in the Spyglass, staring into her drink. LJ might have guessed she'd come here after what had happened on the deck, and she hesitated. Maybe she should go to the galley, lose herself in some baking. But the pantry shelves were already stuffed, and a voice in her head that sounded a lot like Viv whispered that LJ owed Bethany an apology.

Bethany swayed on her seat, and LJ thought she might fall. But she caught herself on the bar with one hand, maintaining her balance by a hair.

LJ slipped behind the bar. "Everything OK down here?"

Bethany looked up at her with heavily lidded eyes. "Oh, sure. I'm just making sure the booze survives the gunfight. It's what I'm good for, isn't it?"

LJ fought a grimace. "You were in no condition to fight, and you know it."

"And you demonstrated that most handily." Bethany reached for the bottle of whisky on the counter. She missed the first time, swiping it on the second, and lifted it to her lips.

"I think you're done, Beth," LJ said, reaching for the bottle.

Bethany swatted at her, but she was too slow. LJ tugged the bottle away and took a step back. She doubted Bethany would be able to get that far in her condition.

"You know what I did for SATIS?" Bethany asked.

LJ froze, still gripping the bottle. She shook her head.

"Yeah," Bethany said, "I figured Viv probably stays quiet about that stuff. I infiltrated anti-AI radical groups."

LJ relaxed slightly. That was something she could understand. "So did I."

Bethany set her glass on the stool next to her, out of LJ's immediate reach, and shook her head. "No. You didn't. You went in all fighty fighty and kicked terrorists' butts. You took down guys who were planning to kill people for the sake of their anti-computer bullshit. I, on the other hand." She laughed, a tear slipping down her cheek. "I infiltrated pockets of people who lived AI-free. Citizens. I was a cook."

LJ wanted to tell her to stop, that she didn't want to hear

the story, but she was here now. She couldn't walk away. She wouldn't.

"The routine was always the same," Bethany said. "I'd show up on their farm. I'd say I'd denounced all my technological ways. They'd take me in. I'd get a job working in the kitchen. And then one day—a week in, a month in, whenever *she* deemed the time was right—SATIS would find a way to spirit all the children away. I never knew if she had a soft spot for kids, or if she was just searching for more candidates, you know?"

LJ nodded, her throat dry.

"Anyway, she'd find a way to get any kids away, supposedly for a night, and that'd be my cue. I'd dig into my little pack of poisons, and the parents..." She made an exploding motion with her hands, fingers trembling uncontrollably. "I poisoned civilians. I orphaned hundreds of kids. So pass me the goddamn bottle, Laura. I've got no room left to regret what I might do if you don't."

LJ had known they were a collection of damaged, computer-raised outcasts. And even knowing that, she'd cast herself as the worst of them, not only because of what she'd done to Conor, but because she had few regrets about the majority of the lives she'd taken.

She hadn't considered that the others might be harboring secrets just as dark.

LJ set the bottle on the counter, but Bethany didn't reach for it. She leaned across the bar and grabbed LJ's wrist, her fingernails digging painfully into LJ's flesh. "If your boyfriend costs us another fight, there won't be anything you can do to save him. From any of us."

Rattled, LJ pulled out of Bethany's grip and left the bar, practically running to escape her. She stopped outside the door, heart hammering in her chest as she leaned back against the wall. Bethany hadn't meant it. She was drunk, and she was sad, and the past had her locked in a grip she couldn't escape. Tomorrow, she'd make some inappropriate joke about them having a catfight and everything would go back to normal.

If only LJ could just breathe.

For the most part, LJ had never had much of a problem setting aside SATIS's more evil tendencies. Bethany was right; the AI had sent LJ to take out terrorists. Even though it lined up with SATIS's own survival plan, the bodies LJ had scattered across the system had belonged to murderers.

And if she'd started racking up that body count when she was thirteen, well, she'd always told herself as she washed the blood off her hands that she'd saved more people than she'd killed. Those people had made it their mission to terrorize the innocent, and when LJ hesitated, good people died.

But Conor was innocent, too. She'd have thought Bethany would realize that.

Voices echoed along the passage behind the ballroom, and LJ's first instinct was to run. But something about the distressed tones made her hesitate, and before she realized what she was doing, she was peering around the corner in search of the source.

Viv and Trelawney stood together at the other end of the hall, talking heatedly. They were so intent on each other that they didn't notice her. LJ couldn't hear what they were saying, but Trelawney reached for Viv, and for a moment she reached back, allowing him to graze her fingertips for a breath of a second before fleeing in the other direction. Trelawney watched her go, running a hand through his hair.

LJ retreated back around the corner, embarrassed at having spied on what looked like a private moment. Viv and

Trelawney? She couldn't picture it. But Viv hadn't shoved him away, and whatever had just happened between them, he'd let her go.

LJ ducked into the first doorway to avoid letting Trelawney see her, before realizing it led her back into the ballroom. To LJ's relief, Bethany was gone, though the bottle was, too. LJ would need to send someone to check on her later, even if that someone was Fay.

For now, LJ slipped back behind the bar and opened the plasteel hatch in the floor that led to the pantry. It was just a tiny storage room with taps, barrels, and glasses, plus a couple of apple barrels and piles upon piles of the bread she'd been stashing here.

LJ didn't need to hide. She didn't need to avoid anyone. She just needed a place to think everything through.

For a few minutes, she just needed to breathe.

11

CONOR

Even without NOA's assistance, Conor had had no difficulty rigging a system to pump the water out of *Robert Louis*'s punctured hull. He was good at working with scant resources to solve problems. Besides, even Conor could admit that NOA had done a serviceable job patching the hole in the brief time it had had to do so before Conor's jammer shut it down. Not that Conor had any plans to restart the AI any time soon.

They could float. And now that Conor was done with the engines, they'd soar. He had to make it to the island in time to intercept his father.

He should have been exhausted from the close call above decks, not to mention ensuring their ship didn't sink and drown them all, but he still had a project to finish before they reached the island. He had no idea where Parker had gotten to—the man was probably tired of hearing Conor mutter to himself over his tech.

The foldout desk in his room was covered in parts. He'd been working with the principles of airlock gel—he'd even managed to procure some for the trip—as a way to get past his father's island defenses. Airlock gel wasn't really gel at all; it was composed of malleable nano-chips that temporarily rearranged the composition of plasteel or glass. When activated, it created a pass-through airlock that allowed ships to traverse solid material without decompressing the bay. Ever so useful.

As far as Conor knew, airlock gel had only ever been used in space. Or space-replicating environments. He thought he'd figured out a workaround, but he wouldn't know if it functioned under atmo until he'd applied it. He needed a way to test it first.

Conor stood, stretching cautiously to avoid enraging his injury. Maybe he could find a plasteel plate in the kitchen. No, not the kitchen; he had no desire to encounter Laura. She'd probably try to take his jammer back. The thought made him laugh to himself; if Laura wanted the jammer, she'd take it, and he wouldn't be able to do a goddamn thing.

So no kitchen, then. There couldn't be space in that cramped galley for all the plates and cutlery. Surely he could find a pantry somewhere.

Conor imagined NOA biting its figurative tongue as he started into the hall, until he realized NOA wasn't watching at the moment. He poked his head into cleaning supply closets and finally made his way into the empty dining area. It was more of a ballroom, really, but a few minutes of poking around led him to a plasteel door in the floor behind the bar.

Excellent. Worst case, he could try his gel on this hatch. And bonus, the beer taps might be operational. He wouldn't say no to a drink right about now. Propping his cane in the corner beside a blue-handled broom, Conor descended the steep ladder, where the scent of apples and spices filled his nostrils, mixed with the promising undertone of barley and hops.

Instead of being greeted by barrels of beer, he found himself face to face with Laura. She stood less than a foot away from him with her back to a stack of shelves, a dim lightbulb burning directly above her head. "What the hell are you doing in my pantry?" she said.

Conor glanced around, then pointed at the barrels propped up along the wall. "Checking the beer supply?" The place reminded him of his father's wine cellar. If the shelves in old Eddie's cellar had been packed with baked goods. "Why is there enough bread down here to feed the planet for a month?"

The last time they'd been this close, he'd asked her to marry him. With Astra heading off to her pilot boyfriend's room, and Conor tasked with helping her escape, Conor had blurted out the question like the fool that he was. Right before Laura'd stabbed him in the gut. Stabbed him. Left him for dead.

He repeated it like a mantra. If he stopped, he didn't know what feelings might replace it.

Laura rolled her eyes and motioned to the ladder, and Conor edged sidewise to let her pass. There was barely enough room for her to do it without touching him, but somehow they managed only the barest brush. As she stepped up, though, loud voices echoed into the ballroom above.

"...just want to talk to you." That was Fay's voice; he recognized it even though it wasn't brimming with her usual rage. In fact, the woman sounded suspiciously sweet.

Laura started up the ladder, but instinct made Conor put a hand on her arm, holding her back. She frowned at him over her shoulder, shaking her head.

And then Fay said, "It wouldn't be a betrayal, Sophie. She's the one who betrayed us."

Laura froze. Standing this close to her, Conor heard the breath hitch in her throat.

"LJ took us in," Sophie's voice said softly, and Laura stepped back down silently. If there'd been any doubt who Fay had meant, it was indisputable now.

"And why did she take us in?" Fay said. "She has her own plans, Soph. You have to see that."

"I will kill her," Laura breathed.

"Somehow I believe that," Conor murmured. He realized he was holding her arm and he let go, but he still stood close enough to smell the herbal spice of her hair.

"LJ wants to use us," a third voice said, and Laura started in surprise. Because the third voice was Bethany's.

Laura lifted a hand to her mouth, her eyes widening in shock. How many of the assassins were convening above them, planning mutiny? That was the right term for this, surely. If Laura was in charge of this little venture, then these women were planning to revolt. He thought of the push and pull between Laura and Fay on deck, and wondered how much power she'd ever had here.

"I don't like to go back on my word," Sophie said, but Conor could hear it. She'd already decided; she just wanted to be convinced.

"None of us do," Fay said. Footsteps paced directly above, glasses clinking onto the bar.

"How many of you are... I mean, how many of us?" Sophie asked.

Pouring liquid. More footsteps. "You're the last, doll," Fay said. "We won't get what we need by sticking with her. She clearly won't do what needs to be done."

Conor had been operating under the assumption that

these women wanted to stop his father from taking over the system. Oh, maybe they planned to kill him for what he'd done to SATIS, but the way Fay spoke, there were commodities involved.

He leaned into Laura's ear. "And what, pray tell, would that be?"

The ship rocked, and Conor gripped the ladder to prevent himself from falling against her, biting the inside of his cheek to keep from crying out as his injury sent licks of flame through his core. If Fay and the others found him and Laura here now... He doubted that even Laura could beat all three of them, even if she made it out of the pantry in time to fight on level ground.

So Conor clamped his mouth shut, breathed through his nose, and forced himself to stay silent.

Laura looked at him, her eyes as impenetrable as the gray stone they resembled, mouth set in a grim line. Predictably, she didn't answer his question.

Fay did. "She promised us access to SATIS. And she might even have meant it. But she hasn't got the stomach to do away with the obstacles."

Access to SATIS. That was why she was so eager to get to the island? They wanted to be under the AI's thumb again? The idea of reactivating the AI that Astra had so desperately wanted to escape made Conor shudder.

He'd known though, hadn't he, that Laura had her own agenda? He just hadn't expected her to sabotage her own freedom this way.

"You mean she won't kill the son," Sophie said.

"She failed once," Fay said. "Maybe she failed on purpose."

Conor had never once considered it. Looking at Laura

now, even with her brow furrowed in indignation as it was, he wondered.

Even if she'd meant to, could she do it again? More than ever, she looked... lost. Though surely he was misinterpreting the shocked expression on her face, the way the color drained away. Still, the urge to brush her streaked blonde hair out of her eyes nearly overwhelmed him, and he had to clench his hand around the edge of the ladder to stop himself. This was madness. Complete and utter madness.

"OK." Sophie sounded sad, but resigned. "I think you're right. So what do we do?"

The ship rolled again, the intensity of the waves increasing moment by moment. An oncoming storm, perhaps.

Above them, something shattered.

"Shit," Fay said, and footsteps returned to the bar. Laura's eyes widened, and she reached over Conor's shoulder to pull the light off.

"Quiet," she hissed as Fay clattered around with a dustpan, glass tinkling as she swept.

"I hardly care to die again," Conor answered. Something about the sound of the cleaning made him uneasy, like he was forgetting something, but he couldn't think straight. The pain in his stomach pulsed.

"Stop saying that," Laura snapped, her voice a harsh whisper against his ear. "You didn't die."

He had, though. "More's the pity."

Where was the line between 'almost dead' and... Well, he was here now, so he supposed that was what she meant. He thought of the minute Trelawney had seen detailed on Conor's chart, where his body had failed and only the return of *Traveler*'s life support systems had revived him. He was missing days, his memories patched between loving Laura and fearing his father and promising to save Astra... and then that blade, hot and sharp, between the old Conor and a cold stretch of darkness that might have contained anything. Doctors, he assumed. Tubes, he knew for certain. His father's voice, lecturing over the vid screen in the corner.

The ship bobbed again, listing drunkenly to the side. Laura braced herself with a hand to his shoulder, pulling away as soon as she was steady.

Conor felt anything but.

The broom noises stopped. And only then did Conor remember what was nagging at him: his cane. He'd left his cane beside the bar, right next to the broom.

"I think there's a storm coming," Sophie said. "I'd better go up and see if I'm needed."

"I'm probably not," Bethany said.

"Of course you are." That was Fay again. "But stay for a sec. Help make sure I didn't miss any glass. Right behind you, Soph."

Conor's pulse quickened. If Fay knew they were there, she'd surely take this opportunity to attack them. Get rid of the problem.

Sophie's footsteps receded. "See?" Fay said. "I told you she'd be reasonable."

Bethany sighed. "Too risky. She might've decided to tell."

Laura's breath hitched again. It had always been one of her tells, that little click in the back of her throat. Not fear or even surprise, but emotion. The woman wanted to deny she had any. That had always been true.

After Laura's fight with Bethany today, she might not be that surprised to find Bethany working with Fay. But it sounded like they'd been conspiring for some time. In spite of everything, Conor's arms itched to comfort her. He repeated his mantra. *She left me for dead.*

"You're probably right." Fay barked a laugh. "Of course, we could've tossed her over the side. Not much opportunity in space to learn how to swim."

"I hope that's a joke," Bethany said.

Laura clenched her hands into fists, eyes flashing like she was ready to commit murder. Clearly, she didn't think it was a joke. At least she had the sense to stay quiet.

The ship bobbed into its highest rise yet, and for a moment it felt like floating in zero g as the bow soared and dipped down to smash between the waves. This time, there was no escaping it. He crashed straight into Laura, biting his lip until it bled to keep from shouting with the pain. She held on to him, and though she was probably trying to keep her own footing, he couldn't help being grateful for her support.

There had to be a sappy metaphor in here somewhere, about the doomed nature of their relationship.

She looked at him for a long moment, and he couldn't begin to guess what was going through her mind. Her lips parted, and he wondered what he'd say if she actually acknowledged what she'd done. If she asked him to forgive her. But she just shook her head and looked away.

"We'd better get up there," Fay said. "This band of fools wouldn't know how to batten down a hatch if it gave them step-by-step instructions."

Bethany laughed. Their voices disappeared, and Conor let out a breath of relief. Fay hadn't seen his cane, after all.

His relief was short lived. It had to be. The ship bobbed, and Laura left one arm under his elbow as if to keep him standing. He wanted to lean into her, to relish the fact that they'd managed to go undetected. His mantra ebbed away, and apology or no, for a moment they just breathed together. He wanted to stay in that moment forever. Pretending.

But that was impossible. Conor took a breath and yanked his mantra firmly back into his head. "You can't reactivate SATIS," he said, drawing away from the ladder. "I won't let you do it."

12

LJ

L J blinked. Reactivate SATIS? Did Conor genuinely think she would? That was *not* what she'd intended when she promised Fay and the others they'd access SATIS's resources. They were supposed to fix things, so they could live their lives free of her influence.

Fay's desire to reactive the murderous AI seemed to fall in line with her continued obsession with the thing, and Sophie clearly thought she owed SATIS her life. But why in the name of Toccata would Bethany... Considering the story the other assassin had just recounted, LJ would have thought the poor woman would be as eager as Conor to jam every AI in the system.

And Conor thought LJ was going to *reactivate* the monster that had destroyed so many lives? LJ wasn't even sure she could. A strong part of her suspected that SATIS's heart had been destroyed, which would mean the AI was gone forever.

He was still staring at her, the accusation in his eyes tallying every wrong he'd endured at her hands, including this assumption that she planned to reactivate her evil AI mother. Part of her wanted to set him straight.

But the other part of her did not want Conor Keyes to tell her what to do. "You won't let me?" she snapped, keeping her voice low, because she really didn't fancy getting murdered for the sake of telling him off. "You can hardly stand."

"I can stand."

LJ dropped her arm out from under his elbow, and he staggered, grabbing the ladder at her back for support. She replaced her hand under his forearm, feeling his muscles contract with effort.

"All right, fine, I can hardly stand," he said. "But you lied to me."

And what else was new? "Did you think we were disinterested? You didn't ask."

He scoffed. "As if you'd have answered if I had."

Derision from the girls was easy to bear. But Conor wasn't a bitter person, or at least, he hadn't been. He'd tried to wield his power, and his genius, to help people. And when his inventions threatened his father's power, Conor had made himself disappear. He'd kept inventing. He hadn't given up. Not until LJ had betrayed him.

She swallowed, waiting to speak until she could answer with the right level of nonchalance. "Depends on my mood," she said. "I'm not planning to reactivate SATIS. I just need access to her network. See? I can be forthcoming."

"Why?"

"Why am I being forthcoming? Maybe I'm tired of you nagging me."

He didn't roll his eyes at the evasion. He just kept those blue gaze trained on hers. "Why do you need access to her network?"

She didn't want to answer that. Every bite of information she gave him was another weapon to be used against her. But if she was going to get him through this—and Viv, too—she needed to show him he could trust her. "I need her money. Dead AIs don't exactly leave wills."

"Surprising. According to Astra, they impersonate eccentric old ladies well enough. Why do you need money?"

LJ tore her gaze from his. She'd never named the bar when they were together, but she'd described it to him in such detail that it was almost a surprise he hadn't recognized it the minute he walked in.

The moment stretched, and she felt his gaze on her face. The electric connection they'd shared since the first time they met still ran like a current between them, but this time she managed to keep from meeting his eyes.

"The Spyglass," he said softly. "You're going to lose it."

He knew she loved it. It felt like an intimate detail to know about her. It shouldn't have mattered, but how many other people knew even that basic fact? Viv made exactly one.

And he remembered the name. That shouldn't make her feel anything but impressed with his memory, but part of her wanted to read into it. To read into everything.

She shut that part of her down. As well as she could, with him leaning on her for support as he was. Even if he knew the truth—that she'd traded his life for her sister's—why would he ever forgive her for what she'd done?

"It doesn't matter," she said. "We're facing a full-on mutiny."

Viv wasn't part of it, was she? She wouldn't betray LJ. And she'd never condone killing people who didn't agree. Fay might be bold, but LJ couldn't picture her approaching Viv with this plan.

"And what do you want to do about it?" Conor said.

"I want to throw them in a cell."

"Don't you mean the brig?"

She glared at him, and he raised his hands in surrender. "Wouldn't it be better to talk?"

She shook her head, incredulous. "You mean sit in a circle and discuss our feelings?"

"Perhaps not precisely, but—"

"You know, you're right," she interrupted, "I think I'll kill them instead."

"You're going to take on a crew of trained assassins, all by yourself?"

It was disconcerting to feel the heat of his body, the way his arm quivered against hers with the effort of propping himself upright. "I'll slit their throats while they sleep," LJ said, trying to shake off her discomfort. "It's no worse than they want to do to me. And you, by the way. In case you missed that part."

If the image bothered him, he didn't show it. He might have been made of stone. If stone radiated warmth. "What about Viv? She wants to save them, doesn't she?"

She'd told him about Viv, too. She'd known better, and she'd told him anyway. And now she was paying the price, in the form of emotional manipulation.

"Viv will forgive me eventually," she said. "And if she doesn't, at least she'll be alive."

And so will you.

With an obvious effort, Conor lifted his arm away from her, gripping the side of the ladder so hard his knuckles whitened. "Blood for blood. At least you're consistent, Lor."

Climbing the ladder cost him. She could see it in the way he placed his feet, slowly but determinedly. She only had a second to feel the loss, to regret the barbs she never withheld, before he was gone. Probably to start a feelings seminar in the middle of a storm. She wanted to follow him, to defend herself, but she didn't know what else she could say.

LJ leaned back heavily against the shelf, massaging her temples. Where the hell had this all derailed so spectacularly? The bottles on the shelves rattled violently as the ship fought for a path through the waves, engine humming with strain. She should probably go back on deck, see if she could help. Or find Viv. Still, she lingered, trying to pull herself together.

A shadow fell across the hatch, and LJ looked up to find Fay smiling down at her. "Your boyfriend gave you away," she said, and for a moment LJ thought Fay meant he'd betrayed her. As much as LJ might deserve it, her throat seized at the suggestion. She hadn't thought him capable of that.

But Fay added, "He left his cane next to the brooms. I knew you were here."

LJ let out a breath, foolish relief flooding through her veins. "Why not kill us, then?"

Instead of answering, Fay pulled a gun out of her back pocket, a condensed Canon40 rifle with an extended barrel. Small. Quiet. Powerful. And there was nowhere to hide. Instinctively, LJ lifted her hands—little good that would do —but instead of aiming the gun at her, Fay blew a hole in the wall above LJ's head. "Whoops," she said, as seawater poured in through the gash. "Hull breach. I'd better seal off this hatch to isolate the leak and save the rest of the ship. Goodbye, *captain*."

LJ threw herself up the ladder, but it was too late. Fay closed the latch, and it beeped in acknowledgment, the digital locks shifting into place.

The air thickened with brine, water lapping already at the middle shelves. She didn't have long. LJ pushed at the door, hammering her fists on the plasteel and screaming for someone to help, but no one heard. The dim ray of light leaking in from the ballroom snapped off, leaving her alone in the dark.

13

CONOR

Conor plunged onto *Robert Louis's* deck as a wave slammed the side of the ship, and the yacht's answering roll knocked him hard against the door frame. Water sluiced over the sides of the ship, clouds gathered above like billows of angry smoke. His wound was a constant burn now, the adhesion pulling like it might pop him open.

Conor allowed himself a moment to hate every single thing about his current situation.

A hand landed on his shoulder, pulling him back inside. Parker was looking at him like he'd gone mad, and maybe he had; he was dripping water all over the interior corridor, drops streaming down his face and gluing his shirt to his skin.

He wasn't sure what he'd been going for out there, only that he'd needed to do something. It had more to do with Laura, with the way she'd been holding him up back there, physically keeping him upright while her double motives came to light. He should have suspected. He should have known.

"I know you're not a fan, but the AI can navigate a storm," Parker shouted, pointing to where Fay stood at the pilot's deck, biting her lip in concentration as she keyed instructions into a panel that looked as complicated as a spaceship's. "Deactivate the jammer, just for a—"

"No," Conor interrupted. "She looks like she has it handled."

Red letters flashed across the control panel, and Fay swiped them away with one hand. AI or no AI, she seemed perfectly capable of dealing with the storm. But she was also planning a mutiny. He limped toward the pilot's deck, intent on keeping her in sight, though part of him wondered if it mattered. Laura and her sisters could shoot at each other all they wanted, as long as he made it to the island.

The thought made him feel like a traitor. To someone who'd tried to kill him. Granted, Laura didn't seem very eager to do so at the moment, despite her wry commentary. Laura might have her own agenda, but no matter how much he railed at her in his head, Conor believed her when she said it had nothing to do with reactivating SATIS. He didn't want to, and it might be just an extension of his foolishness, but his instincts insisted she was telling the truth.

Viv came around a corner at a half run. "Where's LJ?"

"What makes you think I would know?" Conor said.

"What makes you think I was asking you?" she snapped. She was fraying at the edges, a disaster away from coming undone. He could relate. "NOA still isn't answering. Don't tell me you still have that gadget of yours activated."

The jammer pressed into his leg, and he managed not to put a hand on it.

"Wouldn't matter, anyway," Fay said. "The NOA doesn't go searching for lost lambs when the ship is in peril."

The red letters rolled back across the screen. Again, Fay

wiped them away with one hand. Conor frowned, taking a step closer. Was she communicating with someone, or ignoring a warning? Hopefully the patch in the bow was working. His pumps should have drained plenty of water by now.

"Is this peril?" Trelawney said. "How bracing."

Viv pushed through the doorway, hanging onto the frame. "LJ. Where is she?"

The ship rolled beneath them, and Fay smiled. "She's busy."

Conor didn't like that smile. Not paired with the slightest twitch of her eyebrows—he wasn't sure he'd seen Fay look so pleased since they'd met—and the too-casual way she dragged her fingers along the control panel, confidently steadying herself.

Not paired with the fact that she was mounting a betrayal.

Again, the warning flashed across Fay's screen, but this time she was distracted by her own self satisfaction. She whipped around, hurrying to wipe it away, but this time Conor leaned over her to read the words.

Hull breach: dining hall.

Conor threw himself toward the doorway, leaning his weight on the cane and praying the rubber tip was strong enough to keep him from sliding. Trelawney hesitated a moment before joining him, and Conor heard himself shouting for Viv over the roaring of the wind and the pulsing in his ears.

Hull breach: dining hall.

Conor bounded for the stairs, not trusting the elevators in a storm—or Fay to let them descend—half tripping down the slippery ladder as he tore through the ship to the ballroom where the women had planned their mutiny. When he came around the bar, he tossed the cane away and dropped to his knees beside the pantry hatch. He'd left it open when he stormed away after his argument with Laura, not half an hour ago. Now, it was shut fast.

Through the plasteel window, he could see Laura sitting at the top of the ladder, water lapping at her ankles. He rattled the top, and she glanced up, startled. Water beaded on the clear plasteel, giving her a distant, foggy sort of look.

"NOA can open the door," Viv said.

"No," Conor said, "leave the AI out of it. Parker, go to my cabin. You move faster than I do. There's a white toolkit under the bed."

"You're not opening that hatch with tools," Viv said.

"They're not typical tools. Parker, go."

Trelawney ran.

Laura reached up to rattle the hatch again, knocking helplessly against the window. It wasn't right. Once, right after she'd first started working for him, a trio of the asteroid-squatting anti-AI radicals he'd previously tried to team up with—terrorists, and he'd learned that the hard way— had ambushed him on a refuel stop outside Toccata's belt. He'd been on the run from his father, and he hadn't known what he was doing, how badly his shiny ship stood out in the backwaters of the system.

Laura had been the only guard with Conor when the terrorists had caught up with him. They'd tried to make up for his desertion by taking him hostage, and they'd made the fatal mistake of assuming a single female guard would be easy to dispense. They'd cleared the docks, the leader smacking around one of the energy whips the radicals were so proud of—a long, crackling stream of electricity they used to stun, fry, or maul.

But they hadn't stood a chance. Laura had turned the

ridiculous weapon against them, snagging the end of the whip with the practiced twist of a gun barrel that might have been made for that very purpose. She'd flung the energy whip back across the deserted dock with a control even its owner had lacked, severing the leader's neck as she shot the other two attackers in the head before they knew what was happening.

"They'd have used bullets if they'd known it was me," she'd said, grinning as she'd ushered him back onto his pod. "Pity, too. I could have used more of a workout."

Conor's full contribution to the fight had been to slice a cut along the side of his hand as he dived back inside. But Laura? She hadn't had a scratch on her.

Conor hadn't thought it was possible for Laura to look frightened.

She did now. Her eyes were wide, lips parted with the effort of rattling the hatch, but the door was magnetically sealed. It wasn't opening without a command. She knew that, but he could see panic taking over her body, filling her with the need to survive.

He had to keep panic from taking over his, too. He had to save her.

"What the hell kind of tools do you think can drill through a triple layer of plasteel, or whatever that is?" Viv said.

"It's airlock gel," Conor said. "I've been modifying it to work under atmosphere. It'll let her get through the door."

Viv clamped a hand around his arm. "This is not an experiment," she said, pointing at the hatch. "That's my sister. NOA can open the hatch in seconds."

"No," Conor said. He wasn't trusting Laura's safety to an AI. When he was done with his plan, there'd be no more NOA. No more SATIS, no more AIs, period. Humanity would have to learn to solve its own problems. It was the only thing that would save them.

Laura stepped up another rung, head bent to watch the water as it rose. Too quickly.

Viv leaned over the hatch. "If you're just delaying in order to kill her, let me remind you that you're on a ship in the middle of the ocean with a bunch of her sisters. All of whom trained as assassins."

Clearly, Viv was unaware of the whole mutiny situation. The thought of letting Laura drown had genuinely not entered his mind. It probably should have, but it hadn't.

Conor pressed a hand to the window. To his surprise, Laura lifted her palm to meet his. He'd have thought it was just a coincidence, that she only meant to brace herself, but then she mouthed his name. A hot stream of panic unfurled through his chest, and he dropped his forehead against the plasteel window. It might make him a fool, but he couldn't let her die.

She had her head tipped back now, the water lapping at her neck. If Parker didn't hurry...

As though summoned by the thought, Parker bounded back across the dining hall and around the bar, shoving Conor's toolkit across the floor. With shaking hands, Conor opened the top and assembled his materials, unscrewing the bottle of gel he'd been modifying and applying it to the plasteel as water nipped at Laura's ears.

"There isn't time for this," Viv said. "The jammer, Conor."

"No," he said, as Laura pressed her face to the last pocket of air and took a final breath.

He didn't see the knife in Viv's hand until it sliced through his pocket. He flinched as the jammer tumbled out, but Viv caught it easily, snapping the case open and pressing the button to deactivate it.

"NOA," she said, "open the hatch."

The door popped open, water pouring across the floor as Conor grasped Laura's wrists and pulled her out, his wound burning as he fell back with her in his arms. As soon as her feet were clear, the hatch swung shut. The water stopped.

For a second, everything was quiet. Or at least, every*one* was quiet. The storm whipped them back and forth with marginally less urgency, but the wind still bellowed beyond the walls, the sound of the water that had almost taken Laura from him ripping at the sides of the boat like it wanted to try again.

And Laura, she gasped against his chest, water darkening her hair as rivulets streamed down her face, her soaked clothes clinging to her pallid skin. He dragged his fingers through her hair without quite meaning to, not yet ready to let her out of his arms, even as his heart beat to the rhythm of his foolishness.

And then, Viv rocked up onto her heels, staring at him like she might punch him in the face, if his cheek hadn't been resting on her sister's head. "You almost killed her."

Conor wanted to argue, but the words stuck in his throat. Viv was right. He didn't want Laura dead, and yet he hadn't been able to fathom reactivating NOA. Not even to save a life—*Laura's* life. Even now, the sight of the jammer in her sister's hands made him itch to snatch it back and reactivate it.

It was Laura who said, "Guess that makes us even, then," pulling him from his thoughts. She sat up, and he mourned the loss of her body against his as she twisted her hair, squeezing out the water.

Viv pointed a finger in his face, and he flinched. Excellent. "NOA isn't SATIS. AIs are part of the system, and you can't just decide who needs them and who doesn't."

Conor looked to Parker for help, but Trelawney just crossed his arms. He looked like he might be willing to hold Conor himself, if Viv decided to go for a punch. Traitor.

It should be easy to defend himself; his reasoning had always been flawless when it came to the danger posed by AIs. But Conor found himself struggling for a response, unable to deny the fact that despite Fay's assurance that NOA would abandon Laura to her fate to save the ship, the AI had done the opposite.

When Conor didn't respond, Viv just shook her head. Laura laid a hand on her sister's arm with a 'he's not worth it' kind of a look. Well. Perhaps he wasn't.

The storm seemed to be easing off as quickly as it had come on, rocking the ship more gently with each passing moment.

Laura withdrew her hand from Viv's arm. "We need to talk," she said. "We have a Fay problem."

14

LJ

Had LJ been asked to bet on the odds of Conor Keyes showing up to save her from drowning, she'd have come down firmly on the side of 'hell no, he would not.' And yet here she was, *not* drowned, partly because of his actions. She wasn't a hundred percent solid on the details, but Conor had found her. She could still feel the drumming of his heart against her temple, his fingers running through her hair, and if their history hadn't been— well, their history—she'd have thought he was afraid for her.

Viv cast a worried glance back at her as they hurried up toward the deck, but LJ just flashed her a thumbs-up. Yes, she'd have liked a glass of wine and a full day of sleep, not to mention a dry set of clothes. Her shoes squished when she walked, her shirt and pants chilled through and suctioned to her skin. Not ideal, but then LJ was no stranger to pining for things she couldn't have.

Strangely, Conor looked at her as often as Viv did, as if LJ might still drown if he kept his back turned. Since she wasn't sure how to feel about that, she decided to ignore it.

When they stepped out onto the deck, Toccata was already pushing its way through the curtain of storm clouds, sending rays of light skipping over the waves and glinting off the island ahead of them. For a moment, LJ thought her brush with death was making her see things. How could an island be *glinting*?

She blinked, and her vision cleared. It was a dome. The island was covered by a *dome*. It was made of clear glass, or maybe plasteel, and it extended well past the sandy beach, protecting a wide patch of water. It looked like the kind of thing terraformers might set down on a hostile planet or moon.

"What the hell," LJ breathed.

"Hence the airlock gel," Conor said calmly. LJ could only assume the comment had something to do with the stuff he'd smeared on the hatch when she'd been trapped.

"Not that I've been completely upfront with you," LJ said, "but I'd have expected you to mention the moon-sized snowglobe protecting the island."

"I have it handled," Conor said.

"Like you have the AI thing handled," Viv said.

To LJ's surprise, Conor didn't reply. He pressed his lips together and looked at his hands, as if chastened by Viv's rebuke. LJ didn't know what that was about, but she did know that if she'd said something like that, he'd probably have tried to throw her overboard. Tried being the operative word, but still. He'd have tried.

"What the hell," Viv said, "is *that*?"

Because it wasn't enough to have a snow globe protecting the island. The overgrown patch of soil was also guarded by a hulking tower, a cylindrical block of obsidian stone reaching as though to touch the dome that encased it.

If they hadn't been trapped in a storm for the last few

hours, not to mention distracted by pirates and mutiny before that—LJ tried to remember the last time she'd slept —they'd have been able to see the tower sticking up out of the horizon for miles.

"That," Conor said, "is the vault for the island's AI."

LJ wasn't sure when she'd seen a more forbidding structure, anywhere. Anti-AI terrorists hid inside orbiting rocks, so that ruled out most of her tourism experience, and the world Conor inhabited was somewhat more civilized. As long as he didn't go looking for trouble with the aforementioned terrorists.

This tower was a whole new level of Keyes. "It's a fortress," LJ said.

"Yeah, well, Dad doesn't like people touching his things."

"Dramatic."

"You have no idea," he muttered. "Try to mess with it, and the tower self destructs. It's impossible to destroy the heart on this island without destroying yourself in the process."

It sounded more impossible-adjacent to LJ, but she let the comment slide.

Trelawney, who had slipped a thin bar across his eyes that she supposed were meant to be sunglasses, stepped over to join them. "Not to interrupt, but I've noticed it's rather quiet up here."

LJ followed his gaze overboard. With all the excitement of domes and killer fortress-towers, she hadn't noticed the duo of life rafts that were sputtering across the waves, with Fay at the bow of the leader. LJ spotted Bethany's cropped brown curls among the group of about a dozen people, and Sophie's flaxen head.

Fay really had done it. She'd taken them all.

For a moment, the deck was silent. Who did they have

left? Viv, staring out over the water, blinking a little too often for dry eyes. Trelawney, watching Viv from behind those ridiculous sunglasses. Conor, one hand resting on his wound as if in protection. And LJ. The only one trained to fight. How could she protect them all at once? Oh, Viv could hold her own if it came to blows, but in comparison to these women, she knew little more than the basics of self-defense. And Viv was as likely to toss down her weapons in surrender as to fight these particular enemies.

Some army. LJ actually wished Astra were with them. Not just so she could yell at the redhead for leaving Conor's assassination to LJ, but because Astra had defected from SATIS before this whole mess started. She'd be on their side. And that girl could fight.

Oh, well. "We can't let them get control of the AIs," LJ said. "Even if they can't reactivate SATIS herself, they'll look to replace her somehow."

It was hard to believe that was what Bethany wanted, after hearing her story. But LJ didn't know what Fay had said to her. Fay knew the girls well enough to convince them individually. She was capable of telling any lie to get what she wanted.

"Open the dome," LJ said, already moving toward the stern. There had to be another boat, or seven. This yacht was made for hundreds of passengers. Whether SATIS—or Fay—had stocked it with the right number was...well, neither of them operated under the usual societal expectations, so it was tough to predict.

To LJ's surprise, Conor kept pace with her as she moved toward the back of the ship. "I can't open the dome," he said.

"Thanks for saving my life and all, but I'm not up for another mutiny."

"Viv saved your life, not me. And it's not a mutiny, it's

just a fact. If we don't create an airlock gate, they can't get to the island, either."

"Does that dome reach all the way under the water?" LJ asked. She'd lived on Eding all her life; she knew the ocean. You couldn't contain the waves any more than you could trap starlight in a jar. The dome would be built on stilts or scaffolding, something that allowed the water to flow freely. Otherwise, the waves would destroy it.

The ocean ruled Eding. That was the way of things.

"No," Conor said. "It doesn't."

LJ opened one of the storage compartments in the stern and started throwing life vests onto the deck. It was a promising start. "Then when they get there, they'll bail out and swim."

"How do you—"

"I know, OK? I know. Are you in any condition to swim?"

Conor kept his eyes fixed on her, as though determined not to let his gaze drop to his wound. It had to be healing, but it wasn't healed yet, and that was a liability. LJ didn't want to say it, but she wasn't exactly ready to dip her head underwater again, either. If that made her weak, so be it.

"No," he said quietly. "I'm not in any condition to swim."

LJ thrust a life vest at him. "Well, I'm sure Fay is. Open the dome."

She pushed another compartment lid aside. Piles of rubber. Could be rafts, unless Fay had disabled them.

Conor lingered beside her, steadying himself with one hand on the storage box. He looked out toward the dome for a long moment before turning back to her. "I haven't tested the gel yet. It might not work on a planet at all."

LJ unfolded one of the rafts, searching for the control box. Some of these things could inflate themselves. Again, as long as Fay hadn't disabled them. "It's made for space, right? So what's different here."

"Everything."

She snorted. "You're the genius in the room, Keyes. Narrow it down."

He scrubbed a hand through his hair. "It can't be the atmosphere or gravity, because ships emulate those conditions."

She found the raft's control box and set it to inflate. The mechanism still worked, and the boat started to take shape. LJ didn't want to look ahead to see how far the others had made it. "Maybe it likes living between two opposite environments."

"It's not alive. They're bots, so they shouldn't... Maybe it's not supposed to get wet."

LJ wanted to laugh. The only thing that could get them through a barrier to a tropical island, in the middle of an ocean planet, and it was maybe not supposed to get wet? Fantastic.

But she knew better than to voice that. When Conor was stuck on a task, he needed someone to bounce ideas around with, not shoot them down. There'd been plenty of evenings when they'd sat together working through problems, and LJ knew her basic questions could spark something innovative in his plan. It made no sense, but if he had a theory as to what the problem was, he'd solve it that much sooner. That was what he did.

"Come on, genius boy," LJ said. "Might as well try."

Conor nodded, and she could tell his head was already half full of circuits. Of whatever he planned to do next. "I think I'm going to need a cannon," he said, as if he were asking for a glass of water.

Despite the situation, she loved him like this. Distracted,

scheming. Building. It was so different than the way she'd been raised to end things, to tear them down. He bit his lip, thinking, and for a dangerous beat, LJ had to suppress the overwhelming urge to smooth a stray lock of hair away from his forehead.

"A cannon," she repeated. "Is that all? Can I get you a tank? Any other heavy artillery?"

"No," he said, "something like what the pirate had on the schooner."

"Oh, the one that blew a hole in our side? Great."

"I think I can put something together with a pipe."

"Glad to hear it," she said, but he was already hurrying toward Trelawney, shouting a list of equipment he'd need to make an ad hoc cannon to shoot airlock gel at an island-protecting snowglobe. Or so she assumed. Conor had a way of speaking in code when he concentrated on a problem. She could usually make the right connections. She had a lot of practice.

She watched him go, realizing with a start how quickly they'd fallen back into their old way of conversing. Even Conor had seemed to forget. For a moment, anyway. When it came time to build the thing, he didn't turn to her.

Swallowing a wad of regret, LJ finished inflating the boat and lowered it into the water to test its seaworthiness. Fay and the others had nearly reached the dome. They needed to hurry.

After several minutes of scurrying—and collecting equipment—they too were motoring across the waves to the dome. LJ made a point not to look at the tower, but she could feel the thing watching as they hurried toward the island. It made her skin crawl.

They were too far behind. Fay's boat reached the dome,

and LJ could just make out her figure as she dove gracefully from the bow, disappearing under the waves for a tense minute before reappearing on the other side of the wall, her silhouette warped by distance and plasteel. A few of the girls followed, but Sophie and Bethany hung back with the majority. Plenty of SATIS's assassins had been raised on space stations and asteroids. Where would they have learned to swim?

Maybe Fay had enough people. Maybe she meant to abandon them. If she did, could LJ win them back?

As LJ's boat approached the dome, with Conor still issuing a stream of instructions that the others had apparently decided to follow without question, one of the mutineers opened a box in the back of the boat and started handing masks around. Fay had returned to give the end of a rope to one of the swimmers before diving back beneath the plasteel divider. She'd clearly been planning this for a while. She'd thought of everything, except perhaps a submarine.

LJ jumped when Trelawney shuffled up beside her, rocking the raft as he hefted what looked like an enormous pipe over his shoulder. "Water cannon ready. First mate Keyes said I should fire it."

"I'm first mate," Viv said.

"You're captain," LJ said. "How's Conor going to activate the gel from here?" Spaceships and stations had buttons and procedures for airlock gel. Codes. But when she looked back, Conor quirked a smile at her and held up his tab. The boy loved his gadgets. Provided they couldn't think for themselves.

"Just keep it above the water line," he said.

As the mutineers surfaced on the other side of the dome and re-secured their life vests so Fay could tow the nonswimmers to shore, Trelawney aimed the airlock gel cannon at the dome.

The gel hit it in a paste-like splatter, coating the plasteel in thick liquid that looked to LJ like it was crawling rather than dripping along the sides of the dome. It kept coming for a full minute, more, pumping out of the cannon from a tube Conor had fixed to the end.

Finally Trelawney stopped shooting, and for a moment, LJ was sure it wouldn't work. That they'd be stuck on this side, watching as Fay and the others succeeded in harnessing every AI in the system.

The gel spread. Conor hit his button, and the plasteel whitened, exactly the way airlock gel frosted when ships cruised through. "It's flush with the water line," he said.

LJ punched the engine, and took a deep breath. No one living knew what it was like to pass unprotected through a curtain of airlock gel, and she wasn't taking chances.

She'd thought it might feel like a waterfall, but it was more like a quick pulse of energy. A tingle at the base of her spine, and then they were on the other side, shooting across the dome-locked bay with the creepy tower at their back.

The mutineers reached the beach and staggered out of the waves, ripping masks and life vests off as they stepped onto the sand. LJ scanned the group for Sophie's pale hair, Bethany's cropped curls, but the water had rendered them practically identical. She couldn't tell them apart.

Fay, though, was easy to distinguish. She stood on the strip of sand, shouting commands and urging the women toward the line of trees behind them. As LJ watched, Fay turned back toward the water, trusting she'd be obeyed. And then she opened fire.

15

LJ

L J threw herself to the bottom of the raft as Fay's shot cracked across the water, the sound ricocheting bizarrely against the plasteel dome. She half expected to hear the bullet shatter it, but of course Keyes would have designed his shield to withstand gunfire.

It couldn't withstand his own son, but that was another matter.

The others ducked around her, little good that it would do if Fay hit the raft, which was made of rubber and far from bulletproof.

Trelawney powered up the engine, and the boat sputtered forward, launching toward the shore in a wide arc away from Fay. LJ unholstered the Edinburgh and aimed at the beach.

"Don't hit them," Viv said.

LJ didn't respond. The others were way too far away for accuracy, at least with the pistol, but she could lay down some cover, and she wouldn't object if one of her bullets managed to hit its mark.

When she hesitated, people died. Viv should know that better than anyone. LJ took aim at Fay, but as she squeezed the trigger, Viv tackled her, knocking the barrel to the side. The bullet went wide as Fay and the others ran for the tree line, taking them further out of range. The shooting stopped, allowing the raft to hit the shore.

"Viv," LJ said, "they're trying to kill us. We have to shoot back."

"So aim for the water line," Viv said, "aim for the sand."

LJ's mind flickered to bone-dry asteroid caves, shielded with artificial atmo and echoing with the sizzling cracks of energy whips as her prey combed their tunnels to find her.

In her seven years of pre-Conor terrorist hunting, LJ had hesitated exactly one time.

She hadn't known what the other SATIS orphan had been doing there; she still believed SATIS hadn't, either. A girl who'd faked her own death, maybe, somehow disappearing from the AI's systems.

But LJ would always know a SATIS assassin when she saw one. And the girl had recognized her, too.

"I knew it was one of you," the woman had said. LJ could still see her, hip cocked, hair frizzing around her ears in a staticky mess.

LJ hadn't wanted to kill her. She'd hesitated. And she had a bullet-sized scar on her ribcage to serve as monument against that misguided sentimentality. Another inch, and she'd have been dead.

Now, LJ gritted her teeth against the memory and shoved her sister to the side. "I don't shoot sand."

She leapt out of the raft and ran across the beach, firing the Edinburgh toward the trees to cover the others as they staggered across the beach behind her. Viv screamed at her to stop, crying as Trelawney dragged her by the arm, but LJ didn't pause. Bullets sprayed the sand at her feet into little eruptions, and whatever Viv wanted, LJ doubted the other women would miss intentionally.

Fay, she knew, would shoot to kill.

LJ by herself provided a poor shield for the others, but she was better than nothing. The Ediburgh rained fire at the trees as they crossed the beach behind her, and she had to trust them to understand the stakes. Even Conor, who had to be in pain. Even Viv.

Four meters, three, two, and the trees were at arm's length—a preferable fight, if only slightly—when Trelawney shouted. LJ whipped around in time to see Viv stagger, blood painting the sand behind her in a grotesque spray. Without pausing, Trelawney caught her before she could fall, scooping her into his arms while she gasped for breath, clutching her collarbone as blood spilled out of her chest.

LJ fired a last round of shots, and then they were in the trees. She rushed to Trelawney's side, where Viv breathed in ragged gulps in his arms. "Paused to pull my gun," Viv said. "I couldn't... I'm sorry."

Viv had a gun? Flustered, LJ fluttered her hands uselessly above Viv's wound. One of her sister's arms hung uselessly to the side, but Viv knew enough to press against the wound with her other hand. The position was awkward, and her body shuddered with the effort.

LJ stripped to her tank top, stuffing her t-shirt into Viv's wound to staunch the flow of blood. "Pass out if you need to," she said. "It'll be OK."

It had to be OK. None of this was Viv's fault. If someone had to be shot, it should have been LJ.

"There's a guardhouse," Conor said, brushing past Trelawney to take the lead through the forest, bullets still whistling into trunks and splattering into the leaves, but less thickly now. She hadn't seen him take his cane into the boat, but he had it now, plunging into the spongy ground with every step and using it to push his body faster than he should be able to move. The sight sent guilt surging through her, strange and electric and impossible to ignore. She'd done that. He was limping ahead now because she had hurt him, and now he was leading them to safety.

LJ hadn't hesitated. She hadn't paused. When she aimed her Edinburgh, she aimed to kill, even if she couldn't see through the trees. And still, Viv was hurt.

"The guardhouse is up a hill," Conor said, sweat already streaming along his hairline in the thick heat of the island. The trees hovered close around them, roots and vines grabbing at LJ's feet. "Defensible."

LJ didn't want to run—she wanted to end Fay, right now —but she didn't see another choice. They were outnumbered by nearly three to one, with Viv badly injured and Conor still recovering.

They plunged up the hill to the horrible sound of Viv's gurgling gasps—LJ would be shocked if the bullet hadn't punctured a lung—and shouts of pursuit from behind. Sophie. Gretchen. Bethany. Those women had played cards in her bar, eaten her food. They'd accepted refuge from her, from Viv.

She could strangle them all. And maybe she would.

LJ reloaded and took the rear, firing off shot after shot to cover their flight up the hill. "Where the fuck is Astra when you need her?" she muttered, though she wasn't sure precisely what Astra would even do in this situation. Muck everything up. Fail to kill people she was supposed to kill. Fall in love with random pilots. Still, LJ felt the need to blame someone, and it might as well be Astra for not being here.

"And Claire," Viv whispered between gasps. "Don't forget Claire."

LJ had, in fact, forgotten all about Claire Leroux. LJ didn't count her as one of them, even if Viv did. SATIS had taken Claire in so late, and Claire had abandoned the AI so completely, that her existence hardly seemed relevant.

"Don't try to talk," LJ said, embarrassed that Viv had heard her wishing for backup. She should be able to protect them on her own. Not that she'd be sorry to have a pissed-off cyborg on her side right about now.

Ahead, Conor's guardhouse peeked through the trees. LJ had been hoping for a tower like the monstrosity in the water, but it was more of a hut, round stone structure notwithstanding. The tile roof was dotted with holes, and the jungle seemed intent on breaking in. Vines grew up the walls, nuzzling into the cracks between stones. The building had slits for gun muzzles, at least. That would be handy.

Trelawney panted as he carried Viv up the final stretch of sloping ground. Her breathing was still wet, her eyes closed, and anger stabbed through LJ's chest.

Fay might hate LJ, and she might have good reason. But Viv hadn't hurt anyone. She'd only ever tried to help them. LJ was tempted to fly through the jungle to kill Fay now, to end it. She might even have done it if it wouldn't mean leaving the others without a guard.

Conor flung the door open, and they dove into the round chamber of the guardhouse. LJ slammed the door shut and made for the gun slit, forcing herself to stay focused so the mutineers wouldn't have a chance to approach the tower from the hill. Behind her, Viv was sobbing, Trelawney murmuring incomprehensible words of comfort. Fabric ripped, water spilled, and LJ kept her attention on defending their castle.

The mutineers seemed to be taking the hint; the shooting had stopped, and no one followed up the path, though LJ caught a glimpse of a red shirt moving from behind a tree.

With the danger momentarily suspended, LJ turned reluctantly to face the others. Conor was keeping pressure on Viv's wound while Trelawney, of all people, ushered instructions.

LJ wanted to take Viv's hand, but Trelawney said, "We need a fire, and clean water. I have to get the bullet out."

"You?" LJ said.

"I've covered three wars on the ground," he said. "I'm trained as a trauma surgeon."

That was difficult to picture. "Her lung's collapsed," LJ said. "At least, it sounds like."

"Let me diagnose for now, all right?" Trelawney said. "Conor, the fire."

Viv moaned, and LJ's throat expanded until she felt like she might not be able to breathe herself. "Don't let her die."

"I'm going to do my best," Trelawney said with a bite she wouldn't have thought him capable of. He was unspooling a tube from his first aid kit, and LJ found she didn't want to know what it was for.

"There's a water pump," Conor said, startling her. "You could go out. Fill a canteen."

For the first time, LJ noticed how spare their current accommodations were. There was a fireplace in the corner, yes, though she could only imagine the acrid smoke that would pour into the hut as soon as Conor lit the pile of forgotten kindling he was currently sliding into the pit.

There was a bucket, a wooden stool—possible firewood

—a cracked screen by the back window that doubtless didn't work, and nothing else. Just a dusty stone floor with leaves clustered in the corners, the smell of wet soil and too-sweet flowers.

Conor caught her eye, nodding toward the bucket, and LJ understood in a rush that he was giving her an escape. A chance to collect herself.

LJ was split between the desire to defend herself—she shouldn't be undone by her sister's gurgling sobs, not after everything she'd seen—and deep, everlasting gratitude. The latter won out, and she grabbed the bucket.

Hoping no one would take this opportunity to shoot her from behind, LJ plunged out of the sick room as Trelawney unwrapped sterilized tweezers from a slim kit he'd somehow managed to bring in his pocket. It didn't look like it could hold much medicine, or anything useful at all.

The jungle felt too quiet after the gunfire that had followed them up the hill. There should have been birds, or at least insects, but for now at least they were mostly quiet. Something buzzed around her ear, and she supposed that mosquitoes at least were not afraid of gunshots.

LJ moved quietly around the back of the guardhouse to find the pump Conor had mentioned. She took her time sloshing the water into the bucket. It was warm, and would need extra boiling if they really wanted to make it sterile. Was the bucket even sterile? Would a non-sterile bucket negate the boiling? She didn't know.

Viv was the best of all of them. She took care of everyone, sought them out, tried to protect them, and at what cost? LJ thought of the way she'd looked at Trelawney in the hall earlier today—before all the mutineering and almost dying and island hopping—the way she'd let him grasp her fingers for a moment.

Viv wouldn't let herself have him, if he was what she wanted. She wouldn't let herself be distracted by her own desires. All for the sake of her so-called sisters. And in thanks, they'd shot her.

LJ could kill them all, single handedly. Even now, she knew Viv would never forgive her.

Abruptly LJ realized the bucket was overflowing, and she let go of the pump to wipe her wet hand on her pants.

When she had lugged the bucket back inside and set about boiling its contents, Conor sat down beside her. Trelawney had removed the bullet and injected a round of antibiotics—the kit had something useful after all—and Viv was unconscious. Still, it was hard for LJ to look away from her. Should she go to her, hold her sister's hand? She wasn't used to sick bays, unless she was the injured one.

"Thanks for your help with the airlock gel," Conor said. He smelled like seawater and woodsmoke, his hair ridiculously out of place.

It took a moment for her to understand what he meant. Their conversation on the deck of the *Robert Louis* felt like a million miles away. He was trying to distract her.

"I didn't do anything," she said.

He quirked that new, sad smile of his and looked at his hands, like they both knew that she had. The expression sparked something in her, warmth and sadness and longing for what they'd been. But despite all Conor had been through, his smiles had never been dampened before. She'd done that. She didn't deserve even a hint of friendship from him, and still she craved it.

"We used to bring out the best in each other," he said.

Viv muttered in her sleep, and Trelawney leapt to his feet to examine her vitals. Again. Without better medicine,

LJ didn't know what more he could do. There was only worry, and waiting. They were trapped.

"There's no best in me to bring out, Conor," LJ said. "Don't forget what I did. Don't make me what I'm not."

Before he could respond, LJ got up and went to sit with Viv, leaving him alone with the flames.

16

CONOR

Conor volunteered to take the first watch of the night. Parker was exhausted and reluctant to leave Viv's side, and even though Laura had almost died today, she paced between her sister's sickbed and the gun slit, maintaining her half watch until the dark descended and fireflies began to spin drunken paths through the trees. She'd fought it at first, but eventually she'd had to concede that the best way to protect them—to protect Viv—would be to rest. And that left Conor.

So few. There were so few of them, and he couldn't ignore the fact that the others had rebelled against Laura because of him. What that meant, if anything, he wasn't ready to wonder. And she wasn't ready to let him, judging by their latest conversation. It didn't matter. He knew what he needed to do to keep them all safe.

Conor had expected it to take an hour for everyone to fall asleep, but apparently a storm and a gunfight-slash-betrayal were enough to exhaust them into immediate slumber. He himself felt like there was sand applied to the inside of his eyelids. He would have liked to drop off for a while, but he couldn't risk it.

When everyone else's breathing had evened out, Conor picked up his cane and got to his feet, tiptoeing slowly toward the door. Laura slept right beside it, her cheek resting on the back of her hand, lips parted ever so slightly. He paused without quite meaning to, watching her breathe. She looked almost innocent. Certainly not dangerous. He knew she was, didn't need the reminder she'd forced on him earlier, and still he didn't want to leave her. But if he wanted her to survive—and stars help him, he really did—then he needed to stay on task.

It was time for him to do what he'd come for. He had to shut down Eding's AIs.

As he slipped into the night, the damp humidity rolling around him, another figure caught the door and slipped out of the hut. Conor paused as Trelawney joined him, tucking his hands into his pockets and tilting his head back to look at the sky. Conor had thought everyone was asleep, but clearly his friend had outsmarted him.

"I still can't get used to it," Parker said. "No moons."

It was strange. The trees mostly obscured the sky, but here and there a twinkle of galaxy light filtered through.

"I know you want to save him," Parker said, still in the same conversational tone, "but your father will kill you, Conor."

He might. He'd certainly threatened to. "I have to try," Conor said.

Parker lowered his eyes from the sky to study Conor, and Conor saw all at once how fully he'd underestimated his friend. "I don't know what you did that has you hell-bent on this quest for his redemption, but he's not the same as you. Whatever it is—" Parker held up a hand to stop Conor from replying, "—your redemption isn't contingent upon his. You're a good person. Eccentric, I'll grant you, but good. Your father..."

He shook his head, leaving the rest unsaid. Conor swallowed, his throat dry. If Trelawney knew the truth, he wouldn't say that. He'd run as far as he could. "It's as bad as anything he's done," Conor said. "It's worse."

And if he could get Edward Keyes to step back toward the light, to see someone else before himself, then surely Conor had a chance to make up for the lives his inventions had cost. Not only the ones SimuBot had taken on that mine so many years ago—and in the years since, he was sure—but the ones the jammer had cost.

Because Conor stood squarely between two evils. The early prototype of his jammer had been as dangerous as an AI could be. More so, in some ways. But his earliest prototypes had failed because of the System's reliance on AIs, and he couldn't convince himself shutting them all down forever was the greatest evil. Not after learning what AIs could do.

Maybe it was foolishness. Maybe his father really did see people as expendable. Or maybe Edward was sorry. Maybe Conor and Edward Keyes together could save enough lives to account for the deaths they'd caused.

Trelawney read Conor's answer on his face and sighed. "All right. You're going. But I'm coming with you."

"No," Conor said. "Viv needs you. Laura loves her, and I..." He swallowed the rest of the sentence, as if that would hide his foolishness.

Trelawney just twitched an eyebrow. "Careful there, brother."

He thought of the way Trelawney had grasped Viv's hand in the boat, the anguish on his face as he'd caught her on the beach. "Should I be saying the same to you?"

Trelawney grinned, but it was a stretch. He looked tired, his forehead pinched with worry. Conor regretted his contribution to that, but he wouldn't alter his plan.

"Fair point," Parker said, "though I don't think Viv ever stabbed anyone."

Still. She was part of the whole SATIS-driven parcel.

Parker seemed to accept that Conor wouldn't budge on this. Or maybe he knew Viv needed him more. In any case, he nodded and held out his hand to Conor, slipping a syringe into his palm. It was filled with clear liquid, a plasteel cap twisted over the needle.

"What is this?" Conor asked.

"It's a weapon. A last resort, if it needs to be. The closer you hit to an artery, the faster it'll work."

"Fatal?"

Trelawney pressed his lips together and tucked his hands back into his pockets, which Conor read as a yes. He shook his head. "I won't need it."

"Humor me and take it," Parker said. "Just in case."

Conor slipped the syringe into his pocket. Where Parker had procured this, and who it had been intended for—he thought of Laura, asleep by the door—he didn't know. Maybe Trelawney understood this mission better than Conor ever had. Parker had spent his career in some of the most dangerous places in the galaxy, risking his life for the sake of rooting out information. He'd clearly arrived here expecting a war.

With a final glance back toward the guardhouse, Conor plunged into the trees. Though familiar with the Toccata System's cities, he'd been raised in Verity's countryside. Farms. Flowers. The occasional horse, the howl of a wolf or two as they passed through the hillsides.

This wasn't the countryside. This was the jungle. And

nighttime in the jungle was full of the same creaks and rustles and ribbits as the country, plus nocturnal bird calls and disconcertingly large things dodging off the overgrown path before him. He remembered the way to the center of the island well enough, and he didn't dare risk shining a light along the moonless path until he was far enough from the guardhouse to be sure no one was following. He pictured SATIS's assassins surrounding him, watching him pass. Waiting for him to get close before placing a bullet between his eyes. He'd never see it coming.

Even once he did risk lighting his way with a small beam from his tablet, it was not easy going.

For one thing, he'd left his medicine on the *Robert Louis*. Pain meds, healing accelerants, and all. If he'd had them, he'd have given them to Viv anyway, but that thought did not ease the ache in his wound, the skin pulling away from the adhesives as though to rip him open again. He was barely half healed, and he felt it, pain stabbing him anew with every step.

He couldn't move quickly, so he settled for deliberation, placing his cane carefully and testing the ground before him lest he should stumble.

Or get bitten by a snake. Or attacked by a jaguar.

It was slow going.

His father had brought him here on a couple of occasions, back when he still thought they might become partners in inter-system crime. Conor could remember sitting in conference room chairs as a kid, feet dangling as he listened to Edward present ideas that would ultimately earn billions of credits for his investors. Conor had preferred trips to out-of-the-way places like this, where he could disappear into the jungle and make-believe his own adventures.

Conor had spent plenty of time rooting through his

childhood over the past few years, ever since his persistence in designing AI jammers threatened his father's interests to the point where Edward set an unforgivable ultimatum: stop on his own, or Edward would stop him.

Through two-plus years of hiding and acting and digging through the past, Conor had come to the conclusion that his father was bluffing.

When Conor was nine, he'd contracted a fever that resisted traditional medications. He'd been hospitalized for two weeks.

His father had canceled every appointment on his schedule, large and small, to sit by Conor's bedside. It was ridiculous to prize such an obvious sacrifice, or to consider it a shining example of fatherly love. Laura wouldn't think twice about doing such a thing for Viv, after all; that was family. But Conor remembered the worried crease between his father's eyes, the fear Edward had tried to hide behind funny cartoon vids and piles of comic books. The look was etched into his memory.

Conor meant something to his father. Jammer or no, Edward wasn't going to kill him, and that meant there was a chance he could be convinced to do the right thing for the system. With Edward Keyes on the side of shutting down AI technology, the system would listen.

Conor had his jammer with him now, though it was still deactivated; he didn't need to telegraph his presence to his father by shutting off all the AIs in the vicinity. He'd felt bad stealing it back from Viv when she was unconscious, but this was the best thing he could do for her. For all of them.

He began the final descent into the valley at the center of the island, where the white dome of the research hub was nestled at the center of a ring of hills. When he reached the tree line he stopped, pausing to crouch by a particularly thick trunk, as much to rest for a moment as to think. His injury throbbed, tender, along with the rhythm of his heartbeat.

It was one thing to find the research hub again. It was another thing altogether to try and breach it. Solid titanium doors taunted him, nothing that could be breached with airlock gel—even if he'd had any left, which he didn't—and Conor knew there was no way they'd open without the right facial recognition.

When the voice piped into his ear, Conor nearly shouted in surprise.

"Well," NOA said, "what do you propose we do next?"

17

CONOR

Conor muttered a curse. "NOA. What the hell are you doing on my tablet?"

"I don't know what your AI baggage is about, sir," NOA said, preempting Conor's next move—which was going to be to order the nosy thing off of his tablet, "but it is standard protocol for ship AIs to assist passengers during land expeditions."

"Even after they've been asked politely to fuck off?"

"Even after they have been most rudely prevented from operating their own ships, yes. I have opened auxiliary radio channels on your tablet in case of communication malfunction, and I can assist—"

"No," Conor interrupted. His legs ached and he shifted to his knees, though the dampness of the jungle floor immediately began seeping through the legs of his pants. "I'm about to shut down all the AIs on Eding, NOA. You'll be decidedly against that, I take it."

"Not necessarily. If Eding's AIs pose a security risk to the system, I would rather they be shut down. Even if that includes myself."

Hope surged in Conor's chest. He tamped it down. "You're just saying that."

"I assure you, I'm not."

Conor shook his head. After all those years with his father, it was difficult to trust an AI who claimed anything but self-interest. Whatever a computer 'self' might be.

But then, NOA had saved Laura, despite Fay's claim that an AI wouldn't care about a single passenger trapped in a storm. NOA had deemed one life important enough to save. It was one life, one situation, one AI. Still, Conor couldn't discard it entirely.

"I can help you get into the building," NOA said.

"That doesn't sound very legal." Not that the idea of breaking into his father's lab bothered Conor. But it should bother a properly restrained AI module operating in the Toccata System.

"You are the owner's son, are you not?"

"What has that got to do with anything?"

"Are you the owner's son?"

Conor sighed. "Yes."

"Then I can get you into the building without risking legal ramifications."

That seemed like the kind of loophole the Toccata System council ought to close. Did that mean that as Conor's father, Edward Keyes could waltz into any property Conor happened to own? It didn't seem likely.

"You sound as if you've gone rogue," Conor said. A mosquito buzzed around his ear, and he waved it away, irritated.

"You sound as if you're beginning to trust me."

Conor snorted. But he didn't have much of a choice. "Fine. But no flipping. You're on my side."

"I'll hold you to the same agreement."

Conor didn't ask how. He didn't want to know.

With NOA in his ear—god*damn* it—Conor snuck across the short strip of grass that separated the jungle from the lab. It was a white dome that mirrored the clear one above the treetops, assembled with hexagonal panels that looked starkly clinical against the backdrop of greenery.

There were startlingly few security measures in place. The island had been in disuse for so long, and his father clearly hadn't had a chance to get his staff up to speed. No guards, no perimeter, nothing.

The security system on the door, on the other hand, was still fully operational. NOA tried to hack through the locks to no avail, and with apologies; despite his promises when Conor had been well hidden—instead of standing like an idiot outside a set of sealed doors—NOA was a nautical assistant, not a spy AI. He dug into the system in search of a way to fake Conor's credentials, while Conor pressed his face to the glass. If only he'd brought some airlock gel.

"Perhaps we ought to wait until your father shuts the AIs down," NOA said. "The doors will unlock."

"Wouldn't count on it," Conor muttered. "Besides, the shutdown isn't what I'm worried about. It's what he intends to do after that."

"Right," NOA said. "In that case, I've paired your ID with your father's. Smile."

"What?"

A light flashed from a camera in the corner, and NOA tsked in Conor's ear. "I told you to smile."

But after a moment, the door clicked open, and Conor moved slowly inside.

"You could thank me," NOA said.

"See, this is what I don't like about AIs," Conor said. "You say you're here to help, and yet you're the one who's always making demands."

"A little politeness never hurt anyone," NOA said stiffly.

Conor wanted to laugh, and yet... NOA wasn't entirely wrong. If NOA valued human life enough to save Laura's, then NOA could show compassion. Empathy. And besides, maybe it was wrong to try and reason through who—or what—was worthy of basic respect.

AI were sentient. They understood social interaction. Maybe that should be enough.

"Thank you, NOA," Conor said.

"Oh, you're welcome," NOA replied. "May I suggest locking down the entrances to prevent anyone from following you?"

"Can you do that?"

"I can try."

Conor nodded and started inside, passing through a sterile white hallway that smelled of rubber. Inside the white dome, fans whirred above his head every few feet, no doubt keeping the temperature at a premium for computer malfeasance.

NOA, at least, had the sense to fall silent. Conor moved as quietly as he could, placing his cane with care. At the best of times, he was a scholar, not a fighter; right now, he doubted he could win a battle of muscle with a chipmunk, let alone any security staff his father might be employing.

The corridor had no exits, no forks, no options for escape except the one behind him. When he reached the end of the passage, there was simply the mouth to the main hub. It was just a big, wide open room, with two other corridors stretching out from the center like stiff tentacles.

Standing in the middle of a circular console, surrounded by chest-high counters that were lined with screens, was Edward Keyes.

"I hope you're not fooling yourself that you're equipped to kill me," his father said. "Besides, I have a feeling you might need to get in line. I had an ally, but I suspect she may have turned."

Glancing around at the empty room, Conor would have to agree. He stepped inside, abandoning the pretense of sneaking up on his father. He wondered, absently, if Edward was controlling NOA.

"I had the audacity to hope," Edward said, "that you might be the one behind that reporter's ill-conceived expedition." He laughed, still focused on his work. "First, the academy claimed you were at death's door. Then, that you were at death's door *and* missing. You've no idea what a panic you caused those doctors."

With the syringe burning in his sleeve and his wound burning across his torso, Conor cleared his throat. Seeing his father again, it was... He didn't know how to feel, exactly. The man looked harder than he did in Conor's memory, deep lines etched into his cheeks and forehead. "What's your plan?" Conor asked.

Edward glanced up from the console, then quickly back down. "To make sure no AI can ever hurt you again."

He knew, then, that it was SATIS who'd given the order to have his son killed. But it wasn't a computer who'd nearly torn Conor apart.

Looking at his father now, Conor wanted to believe that he meant what he said. Hope sparked in his chest, and he took a few steps forward, letting the sterile light of the room wash over him. "Then shut down the system's AIs, and leave them that way. You don't need to control them to keep me safe."

Edward stopped what he was doing to look up at his son. "Oh, I see," he said. "You want to save me from myself. Or the system from me. Or perhaps both? It's very noble, son. Truly. But who will save the system from you?"

Conor went still. His father's eyes glittered, calculating. "Yes," he said softly, "I know about the radicals you approached with your early jamming prototype. And I know how they used it."

Conor had tracked the cell of radicals from a fueling station between Verity and Orthos, following their decrepit ships out to the belt and their hidey-hole of an asteroid. They'd nearly killed him when he'd landed behind them.

Until he'd shown them what he had. Where his inventions were headed.

Laura would have known with a glance that those people were terrorists. She would have anticipated their move. At eighteen, Conor had thought he understood what he was doing, risks and all. But for all his travels, for all his father's flashy attention, Conor had been sheltered.

The radical cell—the terrorists—had treated him like a friend, like he'd finally landed among people who understood his fears, who took action against the rising threat of AI dominance.

Conor had drunk with them, made plans with them, and had woken one night in a guarded section of the caves to the sound of his tab alerting a news break, the jammer missing from its box beneath his pillow.

The news holos were grainy out in the belt, but the scene was simple enough to understand.

The tourist bubble had been on a gravity-whip excursion around Marya's moons, a gentle rollercoaster of a tour that was something like space's equivalent to whitewater rafting. A little thrill, a little sightseeing, minimal risk. Until the terrorist vessel swung in beside them.

No one understood how they'd done it. Just that the bubble had lost communications, the AI going dark a split second before the life support systems failed. And because the coms were down, no one came to their assistance.

Lying on the rocky floor of the cave watching the news holo, Conor had known. Those were his kills.

Conor himself had barely made it off the asteroid with his ship, earning a broken nose in the process but escaping with his life. He still wasn't convinced he'd deserved to. The terrorists had tracked him—he was a valuable asset, after all—refusing to let him go until Laura entered his employ and they'd decided he was more trouble than he was worth.

It all made sense, now. They'd known her.

His father watched him, as though replaying the story in his mind. His son's great failure, his great sin.

"I replicated the jammer," Edward said, conversational. "Impressive little bit of technology, and I improved on it. It was the work of moments, really, to adapt it for cyborgs."

Conor swallowed. He hadn't considered that. He hadn't considered a lot of things. "Where is it now?"

Edward frowned. "Lost. My colleague in Landry City made some unfortunate mistakes. But as I said, it's easily replicated."

No surprise that Edward had been involved in the attacks on Landry City. "And what do you propose?" Conor asked. "Instead of shutting them down?"

In his ear, NOA hissed, "You promised you wouldn't turn."

Not Edward's creature, then. Or if he was, the AI was doing a hell of an acting job. Conor ignored NOA and waited, watching his father.

Edward said, "I propose bringing lawless planets like Eding to heel, for a start. I propose a central agency for trade. I propose an Empire."

Conor would never forget the mines, the way the frozen ash infested the surface outside the domes, the miserable lives his father had used and thrown away. Because watching him now, his admission about his part in the AI-led attacks on Landry City's glass bridge and opera house, the truth was inescapable. It had been Edward who'd pushed SimuBot to discard those lives.

Conor might not have known how to recognize that cell of radicals as terrorists, but he knew how to interpret his father's words. He knew what an Edward Keyes Empire would be.

In his mind's eye, the system burned.

"And you're testing it on Eding?" Conor said, working hard to keep his voice level.

Edward beckoned Conor to join him at the controls, and he crossed the space to stand beside his father. "See the webbing in the code?" Edward said. "It connects the system. This isn't a test drive, Conor. The council thinks they're so far removed from Eding, but every AI in Toccata will be down in a matter of moments."

"Shut down Eding's AIs, and you shut down the system's."

Edward snapped his fingers, and Conor narrowly stopped himself from flinching. "Exactly. And then we spring the trap."

His father would do exactly what the terrorists had done. For opposite reasons, but on a scale those asteroid-squatters could never aspire to. He wouldn't jam every AI in the system, but guide them. Powerful puppets in the hands of a man who cared nothing for human suffering. Or AI suffering, for that matter.

Conor didn't want to kill his father. Were there another way to stop this, to convince him, to avoid loosing the villain who coexisted with the father, Conor would have chosen that path in an instant. But Edward would never stop. He'd talk his way out of any confinement, use every shred of influence he had to win his prize, to sacrifice the entire system at the altar of his greed, and in one sudden, earth-shattering moment, Conor understood why Laura had done what she'd done.

Whatever SATIS had threatened her with, it must have torn Laura apart.

Conor took a shaky breath and met his father's gaze. "I suppose," he said, "that there would be nothing to fear from AIs if you controlled them."

Edward clapped him on the back. "Precisely." He lifted his hands from the controls. "Do you want to do the honors?"

Conor had spent the last two weeks imagining himself reasoning with his father, explaining the harm he was about to do. In his ear, NOA said, "I must advise against this. I don't trust him, Conor."

Conor didn't respond. It was in the AI's best interest to protest the shutdown. He felt bad about NOA, truly he did, but he couldn't see another road. Once he'd shut down the AIs, he'd deal with Edward. Conor turned his attention to the controls and entered the code his father dictated.

He didn't hesitate before hitting enter. The lights flickered, then went steady.

"You will see," Edward said softly, "that I have prepared for every eventuality."

Conor turned, conflict writhing in his gut, and met his father's eyes. Gray, like his own.

Edward smiled. And then he lunged, pinning Conor back against the console, the motion sending a stab of pain radiating through his core. "Do you really think I don't know what you are? You always had a bleeding heart, son. You never could do what needed to be done."

His father pulled a revolver almost lazily, as though Conor were no threat at all. He was still smiling, as though he had more to say. Another speech, a list of Conor's failings. Numb, Conor slipped Parker's syringe out of his sleeve and popped the cap off with his fingertip, the cylinder warm and solid in his palm.

Before his father could speak, Conor plunged the syringe into his neck.

Edward's eyes widened with shock, and Conor caught him as he crumpled, his wound screaming in protest. White foam bubbled from his father's lips, a stream of blood trickling from his ear as his throat swelled. The poison worked fast.

"I would have tried to save you," Conor said, as Edward's jaw worked soundlessly.

And his father would have drained the system to a husk.

The radio in Conor's ear crackled, and for a moment he thought the AIs were still active somehow, that his father had anticipated his treachery and tricked him.

And then a familiar voice said, "If there's anyone down there, we're trying to land our ship, but ground control AIs just went dark. Which wouldn't be a problem, except we're about to crash into some kind of a dome."

Conor blinked. It couldn't be her. Except…

"Hello?" she said. "Anyone down there? All I hear is silence, but my cyborg friend says she hears someone breathing."

Conor took a deep breath. Things were about to get complicated. "Conor Keyes here," he said. "Is this Astra?"

18

LJ

When LJ woke to find Conor gone, her first thought was that he'd betrayed them. She'd already plunged into the jungle to chase him down—the man left an obvious trail, with the round tip of his cane—when her mind calmed enough for her to remember how well she knew him. And Conor Keyes was not the betraying type.

He'd probably gone after his father. LJ cursed herself for not predicting his disappearance. The man was injured. He shouldn't be limping off to face supervillainous assholes by himself, even if this particular one happened to be his father. Vines twisted around her legs, the damp forest floor tugging at her feet, but she moved quickly. She'd grown up on Eding. The others might have learned to be assassins in space, kicking every which way in zero grav and zipping around in spaceships or whatever, but LJ knew how to track a target on the ground.

Conor had always been an easy one. Still, she couldn't help being impressed that he'd gotten this far, hurt as he was. At least she wasn't following a trail of blood.

Edward Keyes's laboratory looked like a white bowl, spilled and abandoned upside down in the middle of the jungle. Three silvery tubes jutted out of the center, giving the impression of a robotic insect that had been fixed to the ground. Clinically white and blindingly clean, the building was starkly out of place, and exactly what she'd have expected from Keyes.

LJ crept toward the structure, but even when she left the tree line to cross the short pathway between the jungle and the lab, no alarms sounded, and the door opened easily.

She paused in the entry, breathing in the plasticky scent of the place. As a general principle, LJ mistrusted good luck. Edward Keyes was not the type of mad scientist to leave his lab unprotected, which meant something was seriously off here. In moments like this, it was easy to wish for SATIS's voice in her head. Nutjob tendencies aside, the AI had been adept at tracking trouble—even if she'd tended to send LJ toward that trouble, rather than away.

LJ drew her Edinburgh and held it at the ready as she hurried down the hall, the corridor's metal supports rising around her like a skeleton, yellowish lights flickering peevishly. It wasn't entirely unlike the inside of some spaceships. Perhaps Keyes had designed it that way on purpose.

When the corridor spilled her into the main circle of the lab, she stopped.

Conor stood sweating over a half-circle of control screens, talking frantically. To whom, she couldn't say.

Edward Keyes lay unmoving at his son's feet, one hand splayed above his head.

LJ lowered her gun, her heart hammering in her chest. "Conor?"

He looked up, meeting her eyes as if she'd been there all

along. "My father," he said, "he's... He shut down the AIs. I need to open the dome before Astra crashes into it."

LJ hurried across the space and stepped over Keyes's body, automatically assessing the situation as she moved to stand beside Conor. Keyes wasn't breathing, his throat swelled like a purple melon. He wouldn't be jumping up to attack, then. "Did you say Astra?"

Conor flipped a switch on the dashboard, and a woman's voice said, "We're trying to slow our descent, but there's only so much we can do here."

Questions skittered through LJ's mind—who was 'we', and where had they come from, and how did they know to come *here*?—but before she could speak, footsteps pounded from the corridors behind her. She spun, raising her Edinburgh. At the last minute, she swung down to relieve Edward Keyes of the revolver in his hand.

Never hurt to be prepared.

It was Fay who strode into the room, ignoring the guns LJ had aimed at her head. In the corner of LJ's eye, Conor flipped through screens as if nothing had changed, working so quickly that LJ couldn't see how he knew what he was looking at. Astra's voice still buzzed in the background as they worked to open the dome and prevent her ship from crashing into it like a bug on a windshield.

"You broke my tool," Fay said, nodding at Edward Keyes. "I'm going to need you to fix that."

LJ blinked. SATIS-raised Fay, who claimed to love her adopted mother so much she wanted to reactivate the murderous wretch, should be overjoyed to see Edward Keyes dead on the floor. In what way could he be Fay's tool?

"I don't know if you know this," LJ said, "but death is irreversible."

"So you were the ally," Conor said, without looking up.

LJ frowned, but Fay waved the comment away. "You're a genius too, I suppose. You can set up the AIs."

LJ shifted her weight, finger itching to pull the trigger and end this conversation. But Fay skirted the edge of LJ's comfort zone, just out of the range where she could guarantee a lethal shot without a mechanical rest to keep the gun steady. She willed Fay to step a yard or two closer—within ten would be safe—but the other woman was just as well trained as LJ.

"Set them up to do what, exactly?" LJ asked. She might be able to wound Fay from here, but she'd rather not take any chances.

The woman grinned, wolfish. "To obey me."

LJ sighed. "Is there anyone on this rock who doesn't want the AIs to obey them? A lizard maybe? Or are they after system domination, too?"

"Who are you?" Conor said.

The more appropriate question, really. LJ could always count on him for that.

Fay's smile widened. "I'm the sovereign queen of Orthos, fated heir to the galaxy, and the daughter of the woman your father married and discarded like yesterday's trash."

It sounded like madness. Sophie's story about the Orthosan king hung in LJ's memory, and the barely contained anger in Fay's expression as Sophie described her father helping the rebels.

The truth tilted through LJ's mind as fragments of SATIS's past pieced themselves together slowly. They all knew the story: Keyes had promised SATIS a body, tricking the AI into freeing a supposed technician from prison and bringing her to the station—Astra's station—when the technician was in fact a deposed Orthosan princess. Edward had had some plan to marry her and rally her followers—LJ had never been clear on that part, though the man did have a fetish for despotism—but when SATIS learned of the marriage, she'd murdered the bride. Along with all the guests.

Fay should blame SATIS, in other words. But maybe she didn't know. Or maybe her issue was that Keyes hadn't stopped the AI.

"Think faster, merc," Fay said. "Clock's ticking."

Merc. Was that how Fay saw them? But LJ didn't murder for hire. She murdered for survival. "You responded to Keyes's summons," she guessed.

"Very good."

"But you left him," LJ said. "You needed us. Why?"

Fay scoffed. "I didn't need you. I anticipated you. I lost a fight to Astra. And then I lost a fight to Claire." She held up one finger, and then another, as if LJ couldn't do the math without assistance. "So I figured, why risk going up against another of SATIS's protégés—you crop up everywhere, like stubborn weeds—when I could win them over instead?"

And she had. LJ's chest tightened, fear gripping her throat. Fay couldn't mean for the others to fight her. Not here. She didn't want to believe that they would, but whether LJ faced the fact or not, there had been more than one gun shooting at her back on the beach.

Someone had shot Viv. And it might not have been Fay who'd pulled the trigger.

"Where are the others?" LJ asked.

Fay just smiled that giddy smile, her plan coalescing around her as LJ's world disintegrated. Fay might have lost to Astra and Claire, but she knew how to maneuver people. She'd used Edward Keyes like a pawn.

LJ was made of violence, her soul twisted black by the lives she'd taken. She'd expected to meet with betrayal and blood on this island; she was a harbinger of those things herself, a piece of SATIS made flesh after all. She was nothing but a thorn in Viv's quest for renewal through her sisters, a wound that could not heal.

Fay knew that, and she'd used it. To Fay, LJ was merely another piece on the board.

They'd been chasing the wrong enemy.

"No pressure," Astra's voice cut in, "but we're getting close."

Conor pointed to a control panel across the room, and for a moment LJ half expected him to vault over the console railing to reach it, cane and all. Instead, he dropped and slid under it as an army materialized at Fay's side.

It wasn't the one LJ had expected. If Fay still had their sisters, she was holding them back.

But these soldiers were familiar, anyway. Because they were the same pirates who'd attacked the *Robert Louis.*

The one who paused at Fay's side now—their leader, LJ assumed—had a chest like a wall, and she recognized him as the pirate who'd leapt onto the deck of the *Robert Louis.*

At least the pirates weren't wearing their patchwork armor. Thank the stars for small blessings.

"What took you so long?" Fay said.

"The suits shut down," the big soldier said, breathing hard. "We came as fast as we could."

Conor laughed from his station against the far wall, where he was fiddling with buttons—his father had shut down the AIs, and thus the robo suits—and that was the last thing LJ heard before all hell broke loose. The wall-chested man strode toward Conor, probably ready to rip him away from the controls and deposit him in front of whatever panel would install Fay as queen of the AIs.

Instead, LJ vaulted off the platform and landed between

them, the room pulsing blood red in the ring of her peripheral vision. Before the big man even registered her as a threat, she adjusted her aim and fired into his throat, distantly aware of Fay's enraged scream as LJ turned her weapon on the next attacker before a third tried to disarm her by grabbing the gun in her left hand.

She was too fast for him. Rage pounded through her body, thick and hot, and she slammed the barrel of the gun into her attacker's wrist, where it hit the bone with a satisfying snap. He shouted in pain, but he didn't let go, and in their struggle the barrel swung dangerously toward the ceiling.

The soldier bared his teeth and kicked the back of her knee. LJ used the momentum of the fall to drag him down with her, maintaining her hold on the gun and turning it on him at last to blast a round into his skull.

A mechanical whirring noise filled the room, and distantly LJ realized that Conor must have managed to open the dome. Astra's voice faded as Fay's soldiers streamed through the doors, muscular and comfortable with the weapons in their hands, robo suits or no. Conor hit the floor behind her as bullets zinged into the walls, and LJ couldn't tell if his cry of pain was from a new wound or the old.

All she could do was stand between him and an army. This, after all, was what she had been made to do. She'd spent her life battling terrorists in numbers, turning their weapons against them, bathing in their blood.

These soldiers were better trained, but they were slower than she was. And they swarmed her, making it hard for those who remained at the doors to land a shot. Strategy scrolled through her mind as she fought, holding a larger perspective of the chaos that harmonized with knees meeting flesh, bullets singing through bone, the world reduced to the size of the battle.

Rockets thundered beyond the walls, and LJ didn't have time to hope that Astra had managed to land safely. She launched herself at another soldier, surprising him into letting go of his massive stunner and whirling around to swing the barrel of the Edinburgh into his head. The rage beat at her temples, thundering through her veins, and she let it consume her. She was the rage. It was all she knew.

LJ threw a punch at her next opponent. But this one caught her fist, pairing the block with a kick to LJ's hip. LJ moved to the beat of the pain, responding automatically with a sidestep that gave her the second she needed to aim Keyes's still-loaded revolver at her new opponent.

But it was Bethany who faced her now, brown curls plastered to her face, nostrils flared, her lip bloody where her teeth sank into the flesh. Her stance was too wide, her fists clenched, chin quivering with rage or fear or sorrow, or some combination of the three. "Do it," she said. "I dare you."

The rhythm of the battle paused, the room swirling into crystal focus. They were all here now, Gretchen and Tessa poised directly behind Bethany, Ali and Sophie behind them.

LJ was the only thing standing between them and Conor. They hated him, and hesitation was death. Still, LJ didn't move, didn't let her finger twitch against the trigger. She couldn't.

And suddenly there were people storming in from the corridor, redheaded Astra and a tall cyborg with a shock of blue hair that could only be Claire Leroux.

They attacked as a team, flanking Bethany and the other assassins, their stunners dropping two pairs of the women before LJ realized what was happening, her gun still trained on Bethany.

But the others were quick, too. They spun as a group, all but Bethany, who glanced toward the newcomers before returning her stare to LJ. Gretchen launched herself at Claire, but the top of her head barely reached the cyborg's shoulder and Claire swept her off her feet while knocking Ali back with a stunning round.

Claire and Astra fought together, a coordinated pair of blurs taking on half a dozen trained assassins like it was all par for the course. Frozen, LJ watched Astra locked in a fight with Tessa, their blows close and fast, knees blocking kicks and forearms twisting to wrist holds until Astra finally gained the upper hand. She knocked Tessa off her feet and sent a stunner round into her chest.

Astra and Claire obviously liked their stun settings. LJ was only half sure her Edinburgh *had* a stun setting.

LJ was so distracted by the fight, she didn't see Bethany move until the other woman leapt, knocking LJ's gun-holding arm aside. LJ clung to the Edinburgh as Bethany shoved her back, fighting with more strength than LJ would have anticipated, fingers locked around LJ's wrist as she tried to gain control of the weapon.

LJ gritted her teeth, still resisting the idea of hurting Bethany, who was struggling so hard to turn the gun on LJ that she left herself open to any number of kicks. But she didn't want Bethany to shoot her, either.

Bethany's body went rigid as Claire hit her in the back with a stunner round. Her fingers loosened, and she fell.

And all at once, the fight was over. The room smelled like sweat and blood now, the cloying plastic practically undetectable in the aftermath of the violence. LJ took a deep breath, ignoring the nausea that pulled at her gut as the adrenaline drained from her veins, and holstered her weapons.

Astra and Claire did not.

"I guess I should thank you for that," LJ said warily. She glanced around the room, expecting to see Fay stunned somewhere, but the assassin was gone. Of course she was.

Out of the corner of her eye, LJ saw Conor rise, swaying slightly. "It's all right, Astra," he said. "She's not an enemy."

Right. As far as Astra was concerned, LJ was a betrayer and a murderer. With the red fading from her vision, LJ could almost see herself as they did, blood staining her face and hair, bodies littering the ground at her feet. She'd been ready to kill her sisters. She might still have to.

Claire stood unmoving, but obviously ready to pounce if the situation required it.

"She's a friend," Conor said.

Astra lowered her weapon, her expression still icy.

Conor nodded and breathed a sigh of relief. He wavered on his feet, the color draining from his face, and LJ barely had time to dive in his direction before he collapsed.

19

LJ

Once LJ told Claire and Astra about the guardhouse, the two women snapped into action like they'd been working together all their lives. Which LJ knew they hadn't. How they'd ended up together, and here of all places, she had no idea.

While Astra fiddled with the security to keep the assassins contained in the lab, at least until they could return with a better plan for managing a dozen angry killers, Claire lifted Conor from where he'd collapsed—from the exertion, thankfully, and not because of a new injury—and carried him out of the lab.

As soon as they crossed into the jungle, a woman with light brown skin and a halo of spiraled curls fell into step beside Claire to fuss over Conor's wounds, juggling supplies out of a medical kit as she walked backward up the path LJ pointed out. It took LJ a moment to place Isabelle Chagny, who'd been at the Star Leaders Academy, though her presence here was inexplicable.

LJ half expected the school's headmaster to pop up next. Or the Canon System president.

Instead, Astra's pilot boyfriend appeared, looking as tall and tan as ever. At least that made a fair amount of sense.

Claire had no trouble following Conor and LJ's trail back through the woods, which was both comforting and unnerving. LJ kept half of her focus on not stumbling, the aftermath of the battle leaving her trembling with nerves and exhaustion, and the other half on what she could see of Conor. Which wasn't much. Claire might have night vision, but LJ didn't, and she breathed a sigh of relief when Isabelle's ministrations urged him back to consciousness as they reached the guardhouse.

Claire deposited Conor by the wall in the hut while Isabelle beelined to where Viv still lay unconscious on the table, popping the medical kit back open as she went. The hut had felt cozy before, if tense; now, it bordered on stifling. LJ hovered beside her sister, watching as Isabelle gave Viv an injection and handed Trelawney a roll of bandages.

"Don't worry," Isabelle said, when she noticed LJ watching. "This will help."

Viv looked so helpless, her skin ashen in the pale light Trelawney had rigged on the mantel. She didn't look like she'd ever be OK again.

When would the consequences of SATIS's violence stop haunting them? Would they ever?

LJ cleared her throat, attempting to shake off the emotion before it overwhelmed her. She didn't come undone after battles. It wasn't her style. "How did you know to bring medical supplies off your ship?"

Isabelle gave her a little smile. "Where Claire and Astra are concerned? I'd be surprised if we didn't need them."

"Plus we heard a lot of shooting over the radio," Henry added.

If Isabelle and Henry seemed positively inclined toward

LJ, Astra was most decidedly the opposite. The redheaded woman stood in the center of the room, radiating anger as she looked back and forth between LJ and Conor. Not easy, since they were on opposite sides of the hut. LJ half expected her to pull a muscle.

Finally, Astra chose Conor. "You're not dead." She said it like an accusation, jabbing the air with a finger as she spoke and glaring at him like she'd punish him with eye lasers if she had them.

Claire might.

"I...apologize?" Conor said.

LJ snorted, and Astra wheeled around to face her. But Isabelle had finished rebandaging Viv's wound, and she stepped fluidly between them before Astra could attack. "Let's get the full story before we start hitting each other," she said, her voice soft. Somehow, she made it sound reasonable. Like guidance, rather than the censure it was. "What's going on?"

LJ looked at Trelawney, and then Conor, who lifted a shoulder and winced.

"Guess I'm up," LJ said. Astra was still laser-murdering her with those eyes, so LJ kept her attention focused there. "We saw Trelawney's request for ships, so we escorted him here to do his exclusive. If that was ever the mission?"

She looked at Trelawney, who shrugged. Not so much, then.

"We came to stop Keyes from using his patch," LJ said.

"And to use the patch for themselves," Conor said. Because they really needed that clarification right this moment.

Astra flinched toward her, but LJ held up a hand. "Viv and I only want to access our accounts. We're not looking to enslave any AIs to any evil plans. We just want to save our bar on the Archipelago, so SATIS's orphans have a place to stay."

"SATIS's orphans," Claire repeated. She towered over the rest of them, the joints of her metal hand clicking as she tapped her fingers together. "The ones we just knocked out?"

"We kind of lost them," LJ said.

"As it happens, a few of them *do* want to enslave an AI or two," Conor added.

"No big deal," Trelawney said.

Astra cursed under her breath. As if she could have handled this whole mess better.

"Keyes shut down Eding's AIs," LJ said, "and Conor killed him before he could activate his patch. So we have no AIs, but no system-killing patch, either."

LJ glanced at Conor, who looked down guiltily at his hands. No matter how evil your father was, she could imagine feeling guilty about killing him. And Conor, of all people? He had to be completely undone. What had happened back there, to bring him to that point? And where had he even gotten that syringe?

"And Fay is here," Astra said, "because...?"

"She thinks she's fated to be queen of the galaxy," LJ said.

Silence. Under any other circumstances, it would probably sound ridiculous. But anyone who'd worked with SATIS ought to know enough about AIs to figure out how to activate Keyes's ready framework and take over his place in the scheme. LJ had always cracked heads, not codes, but she was pretty sure Viv could do it, even if it took her some time.

All LJ wanted was her sort-of quiet Plymouthtown bar, with enough regular customers to keep the place open.

"OK," Claire said. "So what's the plan?"

LJ didn't have one. She hadn't even known who the real enemy was until an hour ago. She wasn't a hero; she was a bartender who just happened to be an ex-assassin.

"We need the others."

Viv. She stirred on the table, her voice barely a whisper, and LJ was at her sister's side before she even realized she'd moved, Trelawney stumbling over with her. He bent to help Viv sit up, and she let him do it before waving them both away. "I'm OK," she said, though the color was still drained from her lips, beads of sweat popping up along her hairline from the effort of rising. "We need them. Bethany and Sophie, and Tessa. All of them."

"Not Fay," LJ said. "I'm going to kill Fay."

Viv didn't argue. Maybe she thought it would be pointless to talk LJ out of her rage, or maybe she just understood what was at stake here. LJ didn't know how much of their little catch-up session she'd heard.

"We should have restrained them properly at the lab," Astra said. "We left too fast."

"Conor collapsed," LJ said.

"And whose fault is that?" Again, Astra turned on LJ like she was programmed to despise her. LJ didn't blame her. The last time she'd seen the woman, LJ had been rooting for Astra to kill Conor so she wouldn't have to. No one had spelled out the rest of what had happened on *Traveler*, but Astra seemed to have worked out LJ's guilt.

And again, Isabelle intervened. "We need to go back to the lab. We can make sure they don't reactivate the AIs, and we can talk to them. Reason with then."

"Not every situation calls for diplomacy," Claire said.

"This one does," Isabelle said firmly. To LJ's surprise, Claire nodded. LJ had assumed Astra was in charge here; she considered revising that theory.

It was strange to watch the other two assassins follow Isabelle's directions without argument. LJ had thought she was a pilot, not a diplomat in training. Apparently she had many skills.

Maybe Isabelle should be the one to talk to the others. Oh, LJ didn't think Fay would ever come around—or that LJ could restrain herself from killing the woman if she *did* join them—but Bethany might. Sophie might. And if they did, surely others would follow.

On the other hand, Bethany had also thought LJ capable of shooting her. So that could be a barrier.

Isabelle's words dissolved the conversation. Astra and Claire ran back to the lab, while Conor rested and Trelawney attended to Viv. LJ allowed Isabelle to direct her in assembling soup from the nutri-packs she'd brought with her from their ship, stirring them into a basic broth. Filling, if practically tasteless.

LJ delivered a bowl to Viv and they sat together for a few minutes, Viv sipping in silence. LJ didn't know what to say to her sister. It wasn't LJ's fault Viv had been hurt, except that it was, because she'd made enemies of the orphans Viv only wanted to protect. LJ told herself it was pointless to try and talk to Viv with Trelawney hovering, so she sad nothing.

When Astra and Claire returned with reports that the other assassins had vanished from the lab—and that Astra and Claire had done their best to enhance the security to prevent re-entry, though who knew how long that would last —the dinner party scattered to the corners of the guardhouse.

And when Claire and Isabelle stepped outside with their broth, Viv inched her legs around the side of the table and eased herself to the floor. Surprised, LJ offered her a hand.

"I need to speak with Claire," Viv said.

LJ just nodded, a lump in her throat. Of course she did. Claire had been one of Viv's charges, too, and she'd been missing for a long time. LJ watched her go, split between the desire to protect her and run from the gutting fear of almost losing her.

Henry, who'd been mostly silent, stepped over to talk to Trelawney. And Astra went to sit beside Conor at the far wall, bending her head to speak with him. LJ watched them, feeling cast adrift by the murmurs of conversation around her. Wasn't that always the way, though? She didn't fit with SATIS's orphans. She wasn't a genius tech-head, or a manipulator. She'd gone where she was sent, generally without question. Viv might love her, but it was mostly out of obligation, and her sister had more to do than bake bread and hope for customers to show up.

With Conor, things had been different. For a while. With all the secrets she'd had to keep, LJ had let herself be more fully...well, *Laura*, than she'd ever been before. There'd been no terrorists to kill, except in defense of Conor's life. There'd been light and laughter and conversations that had nothing to do with revenge and everything to do with helping other people.

And SATIS had taken it all away from her. LJ didn't want SATIS back, even if that were possible, but she didn't know how to leave the AI behind, either. She touched her cheek, still stained with dried blood, and felt the sudden, desperate urge to scrub it away. Hands shaking, she bent over Trelawney's bucket of water and dipped a triangle of bandage in so she could wash her face.

She couldn't look away from Conor and Astra. If Astra cared so much about him, she should have noticed the way his hands shook, the pinched corners of his eyes that telegraphed his pain. He'd collapsed back there in the lab. He needed help.

LJ scrubbed the bandage over her skin, rubbing until her face was raw. Surely Isabelle would be willing to check Conor's injury. Picking up the roll of bandages, LJ headed for the door to find her.

She was about to step outside when she heard Viv's voice, distraught. She paused.

"I failed them *all*, Claire," Viv said. "Every single one. Except for you, and that's only because you managed to leave on your own. You must think we're monsters."

"I've been a monster myself," Claire said. She was a singer, LJ remembered suddenly. Maybe a famous one? Her speaking voice was clear and pleasant, too. Like bells.

"No," Isabelle protested quietly.

"Viv's right," Claire said, but gently. "A few weeks ago I'd have judged you for sticking with SATIS. All of you. But that was the old Claire. This Claire gets that the past is tricky to leave behind. You don't just hurdle it and keep running straight. It's a loop."

The sounds of the jungle rose around them, chirping bugs and fluttering leaves, and LJ leaned her cheek against the wall, listening.

"How do we stop it?" Viv said.

"We accept it," Claire said. "We face what we've done, and we help each other."

Viv's response faded behind the beating of LJ's heart. She stepped away from the door, clutching the bandages as she turned her attention back to Conor and Astra.

Claire had been adopted by SATIS, too, though much later. LJ knew the basics; SATIS had saved Claire's life by making her a cyborg, and Claire had fled to follow her own mission of revenge after a few short years. Her disappearance had distressed Viv at the time, which was why she'd shared more with LJ than she usually would have.

Even Astra had tried to get away. That was what she'd wanted back on *Traveler*, after all. The reason she hadn't killed Conor, if not the only one. She'd broken from SATIS —perhaps even *broken* SATIS.

LJ had been here thinking it was too late to break free of the AI. But if SATIS still had a hold on her from beyond the motherboard grave, then there was still room to escape. If Claire was right, there was still room to become the kind of person who defaulted to stunner rounds.

And that kind of person might be worthy. Not of forgiveness—it was too late for that—but of a future worth having.

If Claire was right, LJ still had a chance to belong. To redeem herself. But she needed to start by facing what she'd done.

Gripping the bandages, LJ left the door and crossed the room to join Astra and Conor.

20

LJ

Conor's eyebrows twitched in a question as LJ stationed herself in front of him and Astra, stalling their conversation.

Astra, though, slid between them like the guard LJ was supposed to have been. Her expression was a mixture of protective and guilty, like she planned to make up for leaving him alone on *Traveler*.

Something in the way she looked reminded LJ of Fay. She wondered if she looked the same, from the outside.

"If you're so worried about his health," LJ said calmly, "ask him why he's shaking."

Astra's eyes widened a fraction, but she didn't take the distraction bait. SATIS training stuck fast. "And suddenly you care? How long did she have you working for him?"

"Long enough."

"To kill him."

"Does he look dead to you?"

"Nearly."

Conor cleared his throat. "Thanks for that."

Astra shrugged. "Your pride isn't my first concern."

"It's all right, Astra," he said. "She's safe."

He'd said that in the lab, too, or some version of it. LJ wondered when he'd come to that conclusion. When she'd stood between him and an army? Or before that?

Astra dipped her chin toward her shoulder to glance at Conor while also keeping an eye on LJ. A dangerous woman. "You told me that once before."

"This time you'll be in the room," he said calmly.

Astra rose smoothly, casting a disdainful look at LJ as she moved off. As if their chains hadn't been forged in the same fire.

But Astra had escaped. She'd come to Conor for help, and she'd broken her chains despite his apparent death, while LJ let herself fall into the mire. Stay in the mire, even after SATIS was gone.

Swallowing, LJ forced herself to face Conor. He was watching her with that same calm expression on his face, his skin so white she half expected to see through it. Astra might not be able to read repentance on LJ's mind, but perhaps Conor could.

LJ handed him a bottle of water and he drank without looking away from her. When he set it down, she pointed to his shirt. "I think I should look at that."

That. The wound. The last thing she wanted to face, but someone needed to. If it was covered with bandages, she could. She'd give it a quick check.

"I glanced at it," he said. "Looks OK to me."

"There's no way you can really see from that angle," LJ said. She settled onto her knees and reached for his shirt, lifting the hem gently.

The bandages sealed to Conor's abdomen were stained from the inside with spots of rust-colored blood, the edges lifting with sweat and stained with dirt.

"I think the bio adhesive tore," she said. "I need to fix it, and change the bandages."

"Damn," he said, "I thought no one would notice."

The man had the audacity to smile at her. She rolled her eyes and got up to borrow the medical kit Isabelle had left with Trelawney, swiping his bucket of freshly boiled water, too. She pretended not to notice Astra watching her from across the room.

LJ settled back onto the floor beside Conor and splashed water on his bandage to peel it away more easily. With a deep breath, she lifted the corner and pulled.

The gash stretched from Conor's lower left rib and nearly to his navel, a wound that should, by all accounts, have taken his life. It was a stroke of luck that he lived. Though partially healed, the cut looked angry, red from end to end and bleeding through the middle where it had pulled open during today's fight. Without quite meaning to, LJ traced her fingers along his ribs and down his abdomen, fighting the tears that unexpectedly burned in her eyes. She had no right to tears. She'd done this.

"You put yourself between me and an army today," Conor said.

LJ startled, hiding the movement by reaching into the kit for alcohol strips and adhesive gel, which she applied to the open part of the wound with what she hoped was clinical efficiency. Any moment now, he would mention how ruthless she'd been, how many bodies had lain at her feet before Astra and Claire intervened. The look in her eye as she'd nearly shot Bethany. The damage she'd caused.

But Conor said nothing more. He simply watched as she cleaned his wound and applied the adhesive, his breath slow and controlled, head propped back on the wall. Hiding his pain.

When she laid a fresh bandage across the wound and began to tape it in place, Conor said, "Remember the waterfalls on Quin?"

The last time he'd brought up those waterfalls, he'd also asked her to marry him. And she'd answered with betrayal. But the look on his face said he wasn't thinking about that, just the beauty of the place they'd gone to be together before the academy.

LJ didn't deserve to smile, but she couldn't help it. Marya's twenty-fifth moon was a beautiful tropical world, full of secluded vacation villas and quiet corners. "I remember jumping off them," she said. Laughing. Hand in hand.

"I remember hiding behind them."

LJ flushed and fumbled the edge of the bandage, fingers trembling as she secured the last piece of tape into place. She remembered that part, too, his hands on her waist, her back against the rock wall.

"I know you're not flirting with me," she said.

"Sorry. Old habits."

LJ let his shirt fall and started to straighten, but Conor grabbed her wrist. "Stay," he said. "Please."

What could she deny him? What did she *want* to deny him? LJ nodded and settled back against the wall, arm flush against his. He was quiet so long that she thought he'd drifted off, and she was just gathering her courage to look at him when he said, "Maybe we'll go back there one day."

Bitter grief spun sour in her stomach, threatening to dissolve her into nothing. He sounded sad, as if he knew it wasn't true, but she couldn't say that. "Maybe," she said, forcing herself to look into his eyes. "I've got some things I need to make right first."

Conor nodded, somber. She couldn't read minds, either,

but she knew him well enough, the question that salted the tip of his tongue. She could practically hear it echoing across the sliver of space between them.

"It'll sound like an excuse," she said. "If I try to explain. I don't... I can't excuse what I did. Astra got away. I should have, too."

"Astra sabotaged *Traveler* to save Henry's life," he said, "and *then* she got away. She almost took down the entire system."

LJ glanced across the room to where Henry had joined Astra by the opposite wall. Astra had relaxed somewhat, her legs stretched out in front of her. Henry said something that made her laugh. Not an expression LJ would have pictured on SATIS's favorite weapon.

"SATIS used him as leverage?" LJ said.

Conor nodded. And then he glanced toward the door. "Viv?"

He knew her too well. She'd been unable to avoid telling him as much of the truth about her life as she could.

They'd been together on Quin when SATIS broke through one of his early jammer prototypes. LJ remembered the way the sheer curtains drifted in and out of the window like lost spirits, bleached in the reflection of the moonlight-imitating lanterns of the resort. The smell of cotton and jasmine, sleepy bugs chirping in harmony outside.

LJ hadn't known, at first, what had woken her. Conor still slept beside her, hair tousled on the pillow, and she'd sat up with an intense feeling of wrongness. And then, SATIS's voice. Always SATIS's voice.

Now, LJ made herself hold his gaze. "When your prototype failed on Quin, SATIS showed me one of her assassins shadowing Viv. Watching her sleep. She hadn't... Up until that point, the plan hadn't been to kill you. But she figured out about the jammer and it threatened her."

"One point to me?"

LJ's throat ached. She missed laughing with him. "Astra was supposed to do it, but she failed. I tried to get you away, but Viv…"

"She'd have killed one of her daughters?"

LJ shrugged. "Maybe not. But Viv wasn't raised to fight. She was a liaison. SATIS's hands. She wouldn't have been able to… I had to protect her."

Conor leaned his head back against the wall.

"You can't forgive me," LJ said. "I know that. I wouldn't. I chose her over you, and that's it. But I want you to know I'm sorry."

Conor was quiet for so long that she assumed he'd fallen asleep. She wasn't even sure if he'd heard her apology, but it didn't matter. She'd said it once. She could say it again.

The voices outside had grown quiet, even Astra letting herself lean her head on Henry's shoulder though LJ wouldn't have been surprised if she were fully awake and ready to attack at the slightest threat to Conor.

"Laura?" Conor said, and LJ started. She'd been closer to sleep than she thought.

He found her hand and laced his fingers between them, giving them a squeeze. "Astra says SATIS sacrificed herself to save the system. She thinks… She suspects that SATIS saved my life, too." He dropped his forehead to hers, breath trembling against her lips. "Everyone deserves a second chance."

He should be full of accusations and hurt, not stories of SATIS's redemption. If the AI had saved Conor's life, it was only because she'd tried to take it in the first place.

LJ pulled away from him, and the distance opened

between them with an almost physical wrench. Maybe Conor could forgive her, but this time she would be strong for him. She wouldn't forgive herself.

AT DAWN, LJ, Astra, Claire, and Isabelle returned to the lab to track the mutineers. Conor stayed behind with Viv, Trelawney, and Henry. They'd argued for a time about whether Henry could possibly be enough protection in case of attack—which didn't seem to insult him at all—and decided they couldn't afford to leave any of their trained assassins behind to guard. There were only three of them.

LJ and the others found the mutineers on the beach. They approached the camp while Toccata still flirted with Eding's sky from below the horizon, with Isabelle and Claire in the lead, white flags held aloft, while Astra trudged at LJ's back. LJ didn't think flags would stop Fay, though they might give the others pause.

When they arrived, the women were assembled in a semi-circle to greet them, with Fay nowhere in sight. Isabelle and Claire walked until one of the women— Gretchen, LJ thought—called for them to stop, and the two groups faced each other over a short distance of sand and washed-up driftwood. A light breeze shuffled in from the ocean, sending wads of seaweed skittering across the beach.

"We just want to talk," Isabelle said, after a beat of silence.

Tessa said, "Who are you, their lawyer? You're not one of hers. I can tell."

"And thank the otherwise traitorous stars for that," Claire said.

Not a great start.

"Where's Fay?" Isabelle asked.

"She disappeared," Tessa said. Whether they'd elected her spokesperson or she'd taken on the role for herself, LJ didn't know. "She probably thinks we're dead." This, she said with a pointed look at LJ.

They faced off, tension stretching between the two groups. In the distance, the looming black tower sucked in Toccata's rays like a black hole on land, its shadowy profile keeping watch on the island. The sight of it made LJ shiver.

It was Bethany who interrupted the silence. "You're not the problem," she said. "Not the cyborg, or the cute pilot, or the scary redhead back there."

LJ could have sworn she heard Astra growl.

She knew what Bethany was going to say next. LJ wasn't supposed to talk—they were all well aware that she was the problem—but it occurred to her that if she'd somehow helped tip them over the edge of mutiny, she should be the one to speak.

Viv knew them all. She knew their names, and their histories. LJ knew what it was like to end another person's life—dozens, hundreds—and the way they haunted you afterwards. Viv knew their stories. But LJ knew their souls.

"I know," she said, stepping forward to join Claire and Isabelle. "I'm the problem."

She couldn't face Tessa's pouting, or Sophie's teary eyes. Ali wouldn't even look at her. Gretchen quivered with barely restrained rage.

She couldn't face them all at once. So she focused on Bethany. "I screwed up," she said, "but so did you. That bottle isn't going to save you from what you did any more than cracking more skulls will redeem me. Fay wants you to forget what SATIS made you do. She wants you to crave another strong leader so she can abuse you and bend you to her will."

LJ breathed, the air thick with saltwater brine. "I want you to remember what she did, and who you want to be. So we can move forward."

The wind picked up slightly, breathing hot air across the sand, and LJ hoped it didn't mean another storm. She kept her gaze locked on Bethany, her expression as unthreatening as she could make it.

"Huh," Claire said, sounding vaguely surprised. "Good speech."

"That's all it is," Tessa said, but she didn't sound sure. "Words. Meaningless."

Astra definitely growled this time. The woman was half feral. LJ remembered how Astra had climbed through vents to get to Conor's cabin on *Traveler*. Of course, SATIS had telegraphed her plan to LJ, but still. It had been a solid effort.

"Right now, some wannabe queen wants to use Keyes's code to harness every AI in the system for herself," Astra said. "You really want that?"

Orthos. Of course. LJ should have thought of it before. Taking a deep breath, she looked to Sophie. Tears streaked down the girl's face, and LJ knew what she was thinking, what she was remembering. "Fay is the Orthosan princess," LJ said gently. "What was Orthos like, before SATIS saved you?"

It was a gamble. She wasn't sure if Sophie would collapse in the sand and sob. LJ wouldn't blame her if she did.

"I get it," LJ said, keeping her tone as level as she could. If anything, Sophie stood up a little straighter. "You don't want to give a speech. The center of attention sucks, right?"

Sophie laughed a bit, then nodded. And then, with a glance at her colleagues, she crossed the unspoken line in the sand to join LJ and the others.

Ali didn't even hesitate. She holstered her weapon and fell into step behind Sophie, followed by Gretchen and Tessa. A few breaths, a few heartbeats, and only Bethany still stood with her back to the water. Finally, she shrugged and dropped her knife in the sand. "What the hell," she said, "I'm too sober to use this thing, anyway."

21

CONOR

Conor had experienced a number of intense moments in his lifetime, with a high concentration of them having taken place over the last few weeks.

While Laura and the others set out to win over their sisters, Conor waited beside Trelawney, Viv, and Henry, tense with fear, replaying last night's conversation with Laura. And, without wanting to, replaying the moment that had brought them to this point.

On *Traveler*, it had been Laura who'd brought Astra to him. She'd been thinking Astra would carry out her mission to kill him, not that Astra would ask for an escape. When they'd returned to his cabin, she'd been uncharacteristically quiet, jamming her fingers on the buttons of the coffee machine and asking tersely why he would want to help Astra. He'd never seen her cry, at that point, but he'd known what she looked like when she was holding back tears, the way she pushed out her jaw as she pressed her tongue to the roof of her mouth.

He'd reached out to her, traced a finger along her ear to

draw her closer. "Let me build Astra an escape route," he'd said. "Tomorrow, we'll go. Back to the falls, maybe."

He'd expected her to smile at that. She hadn't.

"Anywhere you want," he'd said. "Give up the job. Please."

She'd pulled her bottom lip between her teeth, so close to crying that she would, he knew, soon flee the room. He usually didn't fight that, but he'd tugged her closer and dropped his forehead against hers. Just as he had last night. "Marry me, Lor. We'll go anywhere you want. We'll disappear."

He hadn't even known he was going to say it until the words left his mouth, but it'd made all the sense in the world.

Until Laura'd taken a breath, tears leaking down her cheeks. "Fuck Astra," she'd said. "She was supposed to do this."

Conor had frowned, confused. "What do you mean?"

White hot heat had plunged into his stomach, tearing through the center of his body. He hadn't realized he'd been falling until his knees hit the ground, jolting his teeth and searing the gash across his gut. He'd lifted a hand to his shirt, ripped and wet with his blood.

He hadn't been able to do anything as Laura backed away, hands shaking so hard that she dropped her knife. He hadn't been able to do anything to warn his other guards as they'd entered for their shift change, as Laura's shape blurred around them.

He hadn't been able to do anything but die.

And now, with his back to the stone wall of the dingy guardhouse his father had set up on the island so many years ago, he wasn't able do anything but wait. That he understood her now, at least partly, should make no difference. That she was sorry, that she'd been under the control of an abuser who'd threatened her sister—and that Conor had faced his own such choice when he'd plunged Parker's syringe into his father's neck—should not soften his heart toward her.

But those things did make a difference. And if Laura died at the hands of her assassin sisters, Conor thought he might fall apart. So he waited, with the stone wall digging into his spine and goosebumps chasing each other up his arms, his throat dry with everything he hadn't had a chance to say.

When the door finally opened and Laura returned, whole and smiling, he knew he was in trouble.

They made their way through the forest to the beach, where the tower loomed darkly between the island and the horizon. Claire carried Viv, who was awake and improving, while Laura walked beside them. Adopted sisters, raised in the strangest circumstances. Anger at SATIS pulsed through him, hot and quick.

Before Conor could follow them out of the forest, Trelawney set a hand on his arm, holding him back. A light wind played with the fringe of Parker's peach-colored scarf, igniting an itch of concern in the back of Conor's mind that he was too tired to place.

"In case you hadn't noticed," Parker said, "the guard-house has an open floor plan."

Conor set his cane carefully in the sand, suspecting he would need to stand steady for this conversation. The leaves shuddered on the trees, and his feeling of unease grew. He tried to put a finger on it, but Trelawney was still staring him down. Waiting for a response, though Conor wasn't sure what he was supposed to say. "Sorry you didn't get a better show?"

Though, if Conor were being honest, he'd been a breath away from kissing Laura last night. He would have, too, had she not pulled away.

Parker let go of his arm and ran a hand through his hair, watching as the women made their way across the beach. "What are you doing, man? Do you need me to remind you what she did? Really?"

"No, I don't," Conor said.

Parker sighed. "You never did have much of a middle zone."

Conor clapped him on the shoulder. "Moderation is for plebs," he said. He considered reminding Parker that his own current love interest was, if not as deadly as Laura, probably capable of significant damage. But since Viv had never stabbed Parker, he'd likely lose that argument. "Come on. We're falling behind."

But Parker hesitated at the tree line, and Conor hung back with him even though he wasn't sure he wanted to hear what his friend had to say. "Does she know you plan to keep the AIs deactivated?" Parker asked.

Conor almost missed a step. He caught himself from falling with a hand to a tree trunk. "She doesn't."

The wind whipped around them as if brewing a storm, and Conor frowned up at the dome, the itch in his mind crystallizing. He could understand why the climate-controlled dome would make rain, but why would wind be necessary?

"What will she do?" Parker said. "If she finds out?"

Conor's wound pulsed in agreement, and he tamped down the cautious part of him that screamed Trelawney was right, that there'd never been anything between them and she would hurt him again, if she had to.

Watching her with Viv, though, he wasn't sure he could

blame her anymore. Even if he should. They were both tied to the sins of their parents, weren't they? Conor had invented technology at AI extremes—first SimuBot, and then the jammer—and both had cost lives.

Maybe—he let the thought surface—maybe Laura had made the wound shallower than she should have. Maybe some part of her had intentionally given him a chance to live.

A crack of light flashed across the roof of the dome in front of them, streaming over the water in the direction of the tower. "Did that lightning just strike inside the dome?" Conor asked.

Trelawney shook his head, and Conor wasn't sure if his friend hadn't seen it, or if he was just as confused about why —or *how*—there would be lightning on the inside of a climate-controlled dome.

It was impossible. And besides, Conor had shut down the AIs.

"It must have been outside," Conor said, though it certainly hadn't looked that way.

It was NOA who answered. "It was inside."

Conor cursed, startled, pulling out his tab and holding it up when Trelawney gave him a worried look. He turned on the speaker so Parker could hear NOA, too.

"I shut down the AIs," Conor said.

"I realize humans have an inferior ability to calculate logic, but the fact that I'm talking to you renders that assumption invalid. The AIs *were* shut down, and now they are not. I'm contacting you because there's a problem."

"Because that's not enough of a problem on its own?"

"Something is attempting to corrupt my code."

Dread uncoiled in Conor's stomach. Had Fay managed to get his father's love code working?

"Something?" Conor said. "Like a bad influence that wants you to join the other AIs at a rave? Don't give into peer pressure, NOA."

Trelawney rolled his eyes.

"Your humor always did amuse me, Edward," NOA said. "But no. It feels... It's rather like a virus."

Edward. The AI had called him Edward. That couldn't be good. Another crack resounded through the dome, and this time a shout rose up from the beach. If they hadn't noticed the last one, they'd seen it now. The wind tugged at his hair, blowing his collar up around his neck. "NOA. I'm Conor."

There was a pause. "Yes. Conor."

"OK. So something is trying to corrupt your code. What does it want you to do?"

"At the moment, it simply has me sailing for the dome's gate. There's only one, on the far side of the island. The pirate ship that attacked us on the way here is headed there, too."

Pattering noises erupted around them in the jungle, and something hard hit Conor in the forehead.

"Hail," Trelawney said.

"The queen controls the dome," NOA said absently. "Is she your stepdaughter, Edward?"

The queen. Fay worked fast. "NOA, I need you to focus. You're sailing around to reach the gate. Why is that a problem?"

"Oh," NOA said, "because the guns are active. My mistress wants me to fire on the beach. And Edward—"

"Conor."

"—I don't think I'll be able to resist her. I just wanted to warn you. Before."

Before. Before NOA lost autonomy completely, if he had

any left at all? But no, unless Fay had some reason to warn him, Conor had to believe NOA was acting on his own. "NOA? Thank you."

"I do my best," NOA said.

Conor didn't have time to consider the implications of an AI who seemed to be fading like a forgetful grandfather. With hail pelting his body from every direction, thanks to the wind, and lighting racing across the top of the dome, Conor shoved Trelawney toward the others. "Run," he said. "Warn them. We need to get off the beach."

But Parker didn't have to go far. The women were already running for the trees, cuts opening on cheeks and foreheads as the hail assaulted them. It felt wrong, the ice hitting the hot beach, but the clouds brewing the thunderstorm would be well below freezing, and the dome kept them close enough that the hail didn't have time to shrink before reaching ground.

"We need to find shelter," Laura said, joining him and offering her arm like it was second nature. "We need—"

A bolt of lightning cut down from the top of the dome and struck the water, blinding Conor momentarily and sending a volley of waves rocking toward the beach.

"She's controlling it," Laura breathed. "She's playing with us."

"Maybe her aim just sucks," Bethany said.

A figure strode across the beach from the east, arms raised. Conor would not have been the tallest thing standing on the sand for any amount of money, not with lighting licking at the water and chasing its tail across the ceiling. The others had taken shelter beneath the trees, and though that usually would not be advisable in a thunderstorm, Conor saw little alternative.

Fay moved across the sand with full confidence, unconcerned by the electrical frenzy above her head. She didn't shrink from the hail; she didn't have to. It left her alone, as though she traveled through a protective bubble. She waved an arm toward the tree line, and the hail intensified.

"Well, boss," Bethany said, "what now?"

Laura's gaze drifted toward the tower, and she caught her lip between her teeth, blinking rapidly against the downpour of hail. And all at once, Conor knew what she was going to say.

She turned to face him, eyes blazing. "I need to climb. I need to get the heart."

Conor grabbed her wrist before he knew what he was doing. "You can't. Remember what I told you about the tower? It's not designed for infiltration. It's built to self-destruct. Even if you manage to destroy the heart, the tower will..."

He trailed off, not wanting to finish the sentence, but she didn't look away from him. She knew. She knew, and she was going to do it anyway.

He wanted to tell her she didn't have to sacrifice herself, that there had to be another way. But the AI that controlled the dome, and the weather, had only one heart, and it was at the top of that tower.

Laura used his grip to drag him toward her. "I'm sorry, Conor," she said. "I'm so sorry."

Her kiss crashed into him, reckless and fearless and filled with everything he wanted to say to her but couldn't. She tasted like rain and rosemary, her fingers trailing up the back of his neck, gripping his hair as she drank him in, like this was her last breath and she'd chosen to spend it on him.

And then she was gone, skipping through the forest in the direction of the tower, presumably so she could cut across the shortest swath of sand and reduce her time as a lightning target.

It wouldn't work. Fay would see her. She'd direct the lightning. But Claire was shouting directions, Astra falling in at her side and beckoning the rest of their sisters to follow. The assassins scattered along the tree line, bullets flying, knives tumbling out of practiced grips, pulling Fay's full attention away from Laura.

Fay's bubble—some kind of a shield, he guessed—deflected some of the attack, but she still had to dodge. Her hair whipped around her face as she threw a bolt of lightning at a tree, folding the trunk in half and sending her sisters diving for safety.

Conor watched from the sidelines, numb with fear. Even if Astra and the others managed to distract Fay long enough, Laura was going to die out there.

Parker sighed. "I guess you'll be wanting the lifeboat."

Conor swallowed hard, the taste of the kiss still warm on his lips. "I'll get it. They need you here." He nodded to Viv. "Watch over her, will you?"

Trelawney nodded. "With my life. Good luck."

22

———

LJ

Every shred of knowledge LJ had obtained from growing up by the sea told her not to dive into the water during a lightning storm. Her hair wanted to lift toward the crackling energy above, staticky chills chasing each other along her spine, and every breath felt like a gift as she hurtled through the forest, aiming for the point that would allow her the most direct access to the tower, across the shortest strip of sand. The others might be able to distract Fay for a time, but once LJ's feet hit the beach, she'd be an obvious target.

She wished she'd given Conor a better goodbye, at least. *I'm sorry* could be such an inadequate phrase. She wasn't sure what more she could have said, but *I'm sorry* just felt... lacking. She hadn't apologized to Viv. She hadn't made things right with Bethany.

There was still so much left to say.

If this really turned out to be her last act, she hoped they'd understand. She couldn't take back what she'd done, but she'd give everything she had to make it right.

All she had to do was cross a strip of waterlogged beach,

and swim through the churning bay. While surrounded by lightning.

If they survived this, Conor would need to convince the system council that hiding physical hearts in weird freaking places was not a viable way to keep AIs from going batshit on everyone.

LJ took a deep breath and plunged across the sand. Chunks of ice struck her body as she darted across the stretch of beach, expecting an assault of electricity to take her down any second.

She couldn't fight lightning. She couldn't make the hail bleed. All she could do was run.

LJ's feet splashed into the waves, and she gasped at the cold but didn't stop, submerging her whole body as soon as the water was deep enough. Surely the dome AI could find her, if it wanted to, but swimming underwater would at least hide her from Fay. She swam until her lungs burned, surfacing for breath just long enough to confirm that she was still on course. She dove, eyes open in the crystal water, still expecting to be blinded by a flash of lightning at any moment.

It wouldn't have to hit directly to kill her. It would only need to hit nearby. Anywhere in the bay, really.

LJ swam. Again, she pushed her lungs until she had to breathe, made it halfway, adjusted her course, and dove again. The muscles in her arms quivered, her boots dragging at her feet, but she kept them on. She'd be sorry if she had to climb the damn tower in bare feet.

She'd reached the last lap when the water started fighting back. The tower was within reach, a few strokes away, when a wave rose up from its walls, looming over her head to push back. She didn't know if this was Fay's intervention or one of the structure's security measures. She only knew it was weird as hell to watch the waves rolling in the wrong direction, assembling like building blocks ready to smash on top of her.

The current caught her, dragging her under, and she flailed for the surface as invisible ropes pulled at her feet and spun her in circles until she couldn't tell up from down. Disorienting, like a space walk. She let the current drag her until she located the light, dim now, and kicked toward it.

LJ surfaced, gasping for breath, to find a third of her progress had been lost. The tower had pushed her back across the bay.

She didn't stop to feel frustrated. There wasn't time. Gunfire spat in the distance, the hail still beating at her head, and she plunged under the waves again.

This time, she surfaced farther from the tower than she had the first time. The wave didn't respond. LJ breathed, treading water with her aching limbs, and planned.

Maybe she could approach from underneath. She didn't know what triggered the wave-wall—motion or heat sensors —or whether they only worked on the surface. She had to try.

With a deep breath, she dove. The current tugged at her, but she swam. With her eyes open, she could see the wall of the tower straight ahead, flush against the waves. She pulled past the current, and it threatened to bash her into the tower, but she caught the wall with one hand and held on, climbing from below. Her lungs burned, spots blooming at the periphery of her vision. In another moment, she wouldn't be able to resist drawing breath. And then she'd drown.

She pulled herself up, stone by stone, hugging the tower as the waves tried to wrench her away.

And then her hands met air, and she was choking in a

breath, gasping as she climbed, her body shuddering with relief and the desire to collapse.

You collapse, you die. She would, if she had to. But she still had a mission to fulfill, and so much more to say.

LJ dug her fingers into the cracks between the wet stones, hefting her body up the side of the tower and wishing she had some kind of grapple to swing at the pedestal on top. She'd be willing to bet Claire had something like that. Astra, too. Though Claire could probably shoot it out of her neck or something.

They'd keep Conor and Viv alive. They'd help the rest of the girls, too. If only LJ could turn off the dome. And she had to believe they'd understand, if she didn't make it back, that she was doing this for them. That she cared.

The waves crashed below her, deadly as knives, and she did her best not to look down.

Finally, she hefted her body over the edge, allowing herself a moment to rest there with her cheek against the rock, to look back at the island, where the battle had spilled onto the sand. Lightning ricocheted off the beach, and LJ forced her attention back to the tower before she could count the figures moving across the shore, search for bodies, wonder who might have fallen.

If she focused on the battle, she'd lose. Every breath counted, every heartbeat a time bomb.

The top of the tower was round, with a narrow ledge surrounding a pedestal in the middle. Using the pedestal to help herself up, LJ stood.

The heart lay cradled in a tray of stone, the slim square looking incredibly crackable. How had Keyes planned to get up here, if he ever needed to disable the AI heart?

But that was it. He never thought it might be necessary.

Even after SATIS, the man's self-delusion never faltered. He'd been nothing if not predictable.

How was LJ supposed to destroy the damn thing? If Astra was right, SATIS had blown herself up to destroy her own heart. LJ didn't know of other AI hearts being destroyed. They were meant to be fixed, if something went wrong, not blown to smithereens.

LJ ran a finger along the square, aware of the battle raging behind her, aware of the clock ticking in her chest. As if in response, the tower shuddered.

LJ withdrew her hand quickly. The shuddering stopped.

"Conor knows what he's talking about," she muttered. "You'll take me down with you, won't you?"

Still clinging to the pedestal with one arm, LJ reached into her back pocket and withdrew her Edinburgh. Surely a good strong electrical current could take care of it.

LJ switched the Edinburgh to stun, the lever sticking as she jockeyed it into a position she'd never used. She took aim at the AI's heart, hand shaking. She'd shoot it, and the tower would come down. And they'd all be safe.

"Should've said 'I love you,'" LJ told the heart.

The tower shuddered as she pulled the trigger, electricity surging out of the Edinburgh and into the AI's heart. LJ clung to the pedestal as the tower roared beneath her feet, keeping the round of electricity surging into the thin chip until it began to smoke, fire catching the center as the edges blackened and curled inward.

The world wove, and LJ turned her back to the pedestal. She might never know if she'd saved them. She hoped so.

The tower buckled, and LJ pushed off what was left of the pedestal as she dove through a battlefield of debris.

She hit the water with a shower of bricks, the rocks ricocheting against her arms and legs and sending her into a spin. Disoriented, she kicked, trying to protect her head with her arms while still moving forward. Chunks of rock bit at her legs, and she kept going, trying to escape the whirlwind of the tower's destruction, bubbles disrupting the water so much she could not tell which direction to kick for the surface, or whether she even should.

A brick grazed her cheek and she startled, her lungs expelling a precious breath of oxygen before she could stop herself. She couldn't see the surface, couldn't escape the barrage of rubble that crashed all around her.

She couldn't do anything but drown.

23

CONOR

onor had nearly reached the tower when the whole thing started to shudder, weaving back and forth to expel its intruder. Ignoring the hail that bit at his cheeks, he squinted up to see Laura poised at the top, electricity streaming from her hand and into the tower his father had built.

All at once, the sky calmed. The biting hail vanished, the lighting fading. She'd done it.

The tower swayed, and Laura dove, stones battering the waves around her as she tumbled into the water. One blow to the head, and she'd be knocked out or worse. Heart in his throat, Conor pushed the lifeboat to where she'd fallen, keeping to the edge of the debris field—it wouldn't do any good to sink her rescue boat—as he scanned the water. Stones splashed into the waves and he forced himself to remain calm, his hands gripping the rudder.

There.

He threw himself against the rubber side of the boat, plunging his arms into the still-churning waves to catch hold of her arm.

She caught his hand, and he lifted her over the side, his injury protesting with the barest twinge when he pulled her against him. The fear in his chest dissolved as she gasped into his chest, and he used his free arm to carry them away from the disintegrating tower.

He didn't think he'd ever been so glad to see another person in his life.

"I'm really tired of drowning," she said into his neck.

He brushed her sodden hair away from her face. "Don't be dramatic. You didn't drown."

Laura coughed, twisting her hair around her wrist to wring out the water. She didn't let go of him, though. "Oh, we're joking about this now? That's a good sign."

The sky had cleared back to cloudless blue, the waves calming as the last of the tower crumbled. Conor couldn't take his eyes off of Laura, couldn't stop touching her. She was real. She was alive. She'd been ready to sacrifice herself to save him, to save all of them. "You thought you were going to die up there."

"Yeah, well," she said, and then stopped. With the lightning show halted and Fay's weather powers stripped away, the battle on the beach had stalled. He couldn't make out where Fay had gone. Perhaps into the jungle, to await her plan B.

Because the *Robert Louis* loomed close now, cutting across the waves with clear intention. Fay would have backup soon. She could use the still-functioning NOA on the *Robert Louis*, and the one on the schooner racing along behind it, to activate the ships' weapons and herd the assassins into the forest, forcing them to fight there.

She might be one person, but she was a powerful one.

Conor withdrew his tablet, one arm still tucked around

Laura's waist. Water droplets streamed from the screen as he called NOA.

"Edward?" the AI said, sounding like he'd just woken from a dream. "Is that you?"

"It's Conor. We need your help."

"Conor," the AI said. "Conor. Conor."

"Are you drunk?" Conor asked.

"Oh," NOA said, "Conor. The one who insults me."

Laura laughed.

"NOA," Conor said, "I need you to help me find a way to beat the schooner's AI and fix your programming."

Laura put a hand on Conor's arm. "The jammer," she said. "Do you still have it? We could stop the ships from firing if we turn off the AIs."

NOA made a throat-clearing noise. "Only temporarily," the AI said. "The range on the jammer isn't optimal. But I have a better idea, if you can trust me."

Conor pulled the jammer out of his pocket. It was drenched, but the encased mechanism would work if he activated it. He'd designed it to be sturdy.

But the jammer was a temporary solution. It always had been. If he activated it, Laura would need to get onto each ship and hunt for the AI hearts. It would take hours they didn't have.

And he couldn't lose her again. He'd nearly let her drown back on the *Robert Louis*, because of his fear. If she could shuffle off the weight of her past, so could he.

"NOA has a vested interest in not wanting you to use it," Laura said, as if she could read his thoughts, and the decision on the tip of his tongue.

"He's right about the range," Conor said absently. He pulled away from her, looking up to meet her eyes. "Laura, you should know I was the one who shut down the AIs. Not my father."

She studied him for a moment. He'd always felt like she could read to the bottom of his soul. Trelawney might think she would kill him for betraying them, but he was wrong. Conor knew that.

"OK," she said finally. "And now NOA says he wants to help us."

"I do," NOA said. "Please complete your discussion so I might instruct you before my guns fall in range of the beach."

Laura settled into Conor's side and took his hand. "It's people who cause the problems, Conor. Not the AIs. We need a solution for the Edwards Keyes wannabes of the system, but killing all the AIs isn't going to do it."

Conor didn't quite realize he meant to kiss Laura until he was halfway there, and by then it would have been madness to stop. She tasted like saltwater, and she pulled him closer to her with a hand to the back of his neck.

Nothing about their current circumstances allowed for a kiss like this, but at this point, it was utterly beyond Conor's control. He felt as though they'd just met, the electricity of the first handshake surging through his body alongside every beat of the story that had brought them here to her hand on his chest, his fingers around her waist.

Maybe they couldn't go back to what they'd been. But maybe they could evolve into something better.

"Hi," NOA said, "if I have correctly interpreted the direction of your decision before you distracted yourselves from immediate peril with a potential precursor to sex, I need you to motor around my starboard side."

Conor pulled back reluctantly and kicked the boat into motion. "Promise not to blow us out of the water?"

"I'll do my best."

"Comforting," Laura murmured.

The boat sputtered across the waves, and Conor swung around to *Robert Louis*'s starboard side. From here, the rail guns jutted uncomfortably close, the other schooner rocketing toward the beach from the other side. It might not bother to shoot them at all. It might just run them over.

"Keep going toward my stern," NOA said.

Conor hesitated. "Are you asking us to get between you and the schooner? With all those guns drawn?"

"Are you going to trust me," NOA said, "or are you going to jam me?"

Conor looked at the jammer. It could promise an AI-free solution. But Laura was right; his father had misused AIs to the point of cruelty, both to the computers and to the people affected by them. Conor needed to help solve those kinds of loopholes, prevent further issues.

Trelawney had called him a man who dealt in extremes, but perhaps he could learn to moderate occasionally. Conor threw the jammer overboard, watching as the box arced across the water and splashed into the waves.

"Oh," NOA said, "I'd have advised keeping it as a backup. But since you appear to have made the singularly human choice of letting me symbolize your personal growth, plan A will have to work. If you will please move toward my stern."

Well, perhaps Conor would always deal in extremes. To some extent. Conor gunned the motorboat between the two ships. "And plan A would be?"

"Oh," NOA said, "that's simple. You're bait."

NOA's guns fired. Smoke arched across the water, and Laura jumped as the torpedos split the schooner's hull. A beat, and the ship exploded, shards of metal and plasteel shooting toward the dome with blasts of smoke and flame. Conor didn't know what sensitive part of the ship NOA had known to aim for, but the AI had been true.

"Now, Edward," NOA said, as the acrid scent of the smoke curled into Conor's nostrils, "I'm going to need you to run."

24

LJ

They arrived on the shore as NOA turned the guns on his own decks, plumes of smoke billowing into the air as the deck split, the bow dipping uselessly into the waves. LJ looked at Conor and tapped her ear. Maybe NOA could have survived, could still be out there somewhere. But Conor just shook his head and squeezed her hand. He was looking back at the ship like he'd lost a friend.

She couldn't believe he'd trusted NOA to help them, let alone tossed the jammer.

Astra met them at the beach and helped tow the boat onto the sand, a move LJ appreciated. Her own limbs were shaky and raw after the desperate swim, her ankle smarting where a stone had cracked into her during the dive. Between the adrenaline of falling and everything else, she hadn't noticed the pain until she'd tried to put weight on it.

"Huh," Astra said. "Explosions look different in atmo."

"Why do all your AIs feel the need to blow themselves up?" Isabelle said, dashing in next to Astra to pull the boat out of LJ's hands. "Isn't there another way for them to destroy their hearts?"

"I'll put it on my to-do list," Conor said. He was still gazing out toward the burning ship, his eyes moist with tears. NOA really was gone, then.

And Conor must be thinking of helping the council with their AI troubles. A new world order, one LJ could get behind.

"I saw lightning hit the shore," LJ said, turning to the group of women who trotted across the sand to join her. Bethany, Sophie, Ali, Tessa, Gretchen. And behind them, Viv, moving slowly with Parker Trelawney at her side.

Apparently that really was going to be a thing.

"Everyone's OK," Astra said.

"Bad aim?" LJ asked. Astra just shrugged, and LJ understood. Battles were chaos.

And this one wasn't over. Across the beach, Fay stumbled out of the trees with her arms raised.

"We could leave her here," Astra suggested. "Burn down the lab, cut off her escape routes."

LJ drew the Edinburgh, soaked but hopefully still operational. She didn't raise it, even as Fay trudged across the sand, looking pale and defeated.

"Everyone deserves a second chance," LJ said.

"She'll try to attack us," Claire said. "That one will fight to the last."

Fay got within a few feet of them and stopped, surveying the group of assassins who stood together by the water's edge. "You disgrace her," she said, but she sounded tired. "She saved you all, and this is how you repay her?"

"SATIS abused us," LJ said. "We're only together because she's dead. And she murdered your mother. You have to know that."

Maybe Fay knew it, or maybe she'd pushed the suspicion so far within that she'd never be able to extract it. Fay bared her teeth. "Edward Keyes—"

"Abandoned your mother after marrying her, sure," LJ said. "No one's absolving him. But it was SATIS who killed the life support on the original station. SATIS who left her to die. Maybe she kept the truth from you, but she showed it to us."

The image was seared into LJ's memory: Edward Keyes, donning that oxygen mask as he sauntered away from his suffocating bride and their wedding guests. SATIS played it with bitter rage, caught between regret and heartache, but LJ and Viv had grown up viewing it with horror.

Fay's eyes darted along the line of women, and LJ didn't have to look back at them to know they were confirming her story. Fay shook her head, refusing to believe. SATIS must have spun the bride's daughter a different tale.

LJ read the twitch of muscle in her jaw, the barest shift of her weight that accompanied the last shred of desperation in her eyes, and she knew Fay was about to leap before the other woman launched herself at LJ.

LJ understood. She could even empathize. Sometimes, it was too impossible to face the pain of your own redemption.

But LJ was ready. With her Edinburgh set to stun, she fired, and Fay crumpled into a heap in the sand.

"Huh," LJ said, holstering the pistol. "Stunners really do work. Good to know."

ENDING a battle was supposed to be the hard part, but there were logistics to manage in transporting twenty-odd people back to the Archipelago, given that they'd blown up their ship, and Astra's space pod could fit no more than five cramped passengers.

So Isabelle piloted the pod back to the Archipelago with Viv, who needed medical care, plus Astra escorting Fay, and, finally, Henry—who could then pilot Conor's much-bigger pod back to the island to pick up the rest.

It'd taken several days to reach the island by sea. A few hours in the air, and they'd be home.

While they waited, Conor and Trelawney went to the lab to make sure the system's AIs regained their autonomy, and LJ found Bethany sitting alone in the sand with her knees drawn to her chest, looking out at the bay. The waves were gentle again, the sky clear, as though there'd never been an angry storm beating at the top of the dome. LJ sat beside her, and they watched the water in silence for a few long minutes.

"It's nice here," Bethany said after a while. "As long as no one's trying to kill us. Does Conor own this island or something? Maybe we could build a resort here. We'll have to pop off that dome though."

LJ smiled. "I have no idea if he owns it."

Bethany brushed a wayward curl out of her eyes. "I don't know where I belong now. I yelled at you for not dealing with your issues or whatever, but I kept myself separate, too."

LJ hadn't really considered it before, how Bethany had stationed herself on that barstool while the others bonded over poker and bickered over seating arrangements. She thought of what Claire had told Viv outside the hut last night, how change had to be more than a hurdle to jump, how facing what they'd done was a daily battle.

Until one day, maybe, the pain would ebb. LJ had to believe it would.

"I don't think we can get better in a day," LJ said. "We can't expect it of ourselves, and we shouldn't expect it of each other, either. I'm sorry, Bethany."

Bethany snorted. "Why? I'm the one who betrayed you and kinda sorta tried to kill you."

"Because I didn't get it," LJ said. "I didn't value this. Us."

Bethany propped an arm awkwardly around LJ's shoulders. "So what now?"

"Come back to the Spyglass," LJ said. "Help Viv and me out. We can cook and go fishing and I don't know, brawl with pirates if we get bored."

Bethany laughed, but she didn't respond right away. She tapped her fingers on LJ's shoulder, her expression lost in thought, and for a moment LJ thought she might refuse. What would that look like? If all the women left?

"All right," Bethany said finally. "But would you consider turning the place into a bakery?"

EPILOGUE

LJ

Heroic feats, LJ thought, should be properly celebrated. But Conor had spent only a single night on the Archipelago before jaunting off to counsel the council, while several of the girls—including Sophie—escorted Fay to Orthos for trial, and Viv's wounds had left her in need of quiet recovery time.

LJ had spent weeks wishing the Spyglass would quiet down so she could attract customers again, and now all she wanted were corners stuffed with her bickering sisters. And maybe—she'd barely allowed herself to contemplate it—a basement with tables covered in wires and gears, Conor bending over some new invention.

But now that Sophie and the others had returned, Astra and Claire would be leaving. Astra to Verity with Henry, supposedly for some peace and quiet—though that was difficult to picture—Claire and Iz to scour the system, and those nearby, for more SATIS orphans.

"At least we'll still have enough of a crowd to keep us occupied," LJ said to Viv as they leaned on the bar together, watching the girls. Together, for one more evening.

"You will," Viv said.

LJ looked at her sister, the full truth mirrored in Viv's eyes. "You're leaving, too."

Viv nodded. "Parker and I are going with Claire and Iz. They invited us along, and I just... There are still over a dozen girls out there somewhere."

"Plus," LJ said, "maybe there'll be a bit of adventure in it?"

Viv grinned. "You're not mad?"

LJ grabbed her sister's hand and squeezed. "At you? Never."

Bethany waltzed by, carrying a tray. "You've still got me," she said, winking.

"Yeah, I know. I'll have to fumigate to get you out of here," LJ said.

Bethany stuck her tongue out and kept moving, bypassing the bar to join the others at cards.

When the door opened, revealing Eding's early evening shuffle of activity, LJ had to stop herself from leaping over the counter to greet Conor. He carried his cane, though he wasn't using it at the moment, and his posture was beginning to straighten back to its former strength.

LJ restrained herself, waiting until he'd dropped his bag on a stool and come around the bar. "Well," he said, "they listened. There's a committee, and I'm on it, and it's absolutely horrible."

He wrinkled his nose, but LJ thought he was pleased.

"I was thinking," she said, "that you might be able to manage most of your committee responsibilities from Eding."

He tucked a strand of her hair behind her ear. "Oh? I didn't realize Eding featured such modern technology as vid chats."

"Sure it does," she said, playing along, "and besides, you did recently purchase a bar here."

LJ's inheritance might have remained MIA, but Conor's hadn't.

"I *invested* in a bar," he said. "The Spyglass will always be yours."

"And you plan to be a silent partner? Or maybe an invisible one?"

She said it like a joke, but she felt the question tightening around her throat. Conor had transferred the money before he left, but in spite of everything, she'd half expected him not to return from his trip. She wouldn't have blamed him, had he decided to stay away.

"Oh, definitely not," he said, glancing around the room. "You know how opinionated I am. We need to add pink curtains to every window. Scented candles on the tables. Glitter for the sign. And maybe a unicorn."

LJ grimaced. "On second thought, maybe you should get out."

He kissed her, and she felt the promise in it. She couldn't be sure he wouldn't wake up one day to realize he couldn't actually forgive her for what she'd done, but he was willing to try. And so was she.

"Never," he said, and kissed her again. "Now if you'll excuse me, I believe two of your terrifying sisters are waiting to speak with you. I should drop my things upstairs."

She watched him go, leaning her elbows on the bar as Astra and Claire settled onto stools across from her. She half thought they'd come to yell at her about something, or maybe threaten her with bodily harm if she hurt Conor again, but they just sat there, looking all companionable and strangely friendly. She wouldn't have expected it to suit them, but it did.

"Rum?" LJ asked.

Claire shrugged and leaned her metal arm on the table. "Doesn't really affect me, but OK."

Astra frowned. "Champagne?"

"This look like the kind of place that serves champagne?"

Astra shook her head. "Give Conor a month, and you'll be stocking the best."

LJ grinned. "He can try." She dashed a healthy pour of her best spiced rum into three glasses, and they drank quietly for a moment, looking around. The girls were arguing over their poker game, as usual, but LJ didn't feel the need to intervene. "So, I guess this is it. No more Keyes. Fresh start, separate ways, all that stuff."

"We'll see each other," Claire said.

"Speak for yourself," Astra said. "Unless you're planning to visit Verity. I'm not heading back into space for a while."

"We'll visit," LJ said.

Astra raised her glass. LJ and Claire toasted her, and LJ couldn't help thinking that SATIS had, unwittingly, done one very good thing. Maybe she'd sacrificed herself to fix what she'd done, and maybe she'd even saved Conor's life as Astra suspected. And when SATIS had sacrificed herself, she'd set off a chain of events she couldn't have anticipated. She'd brought her daughters together.

If nothing else, LJ could drink to that.

～

THE END

～

NEWSLETTER

Thanks for reading! I hope you enjoyed reading the Toccata System trilogy as much as I enjoyed writing it.

If you'd like to hang out in Toccata a little longer, you can join my newsletter and get a free story collection, which includes a Toccata System prequel story. Visit http://katesheeranswed.com/free-books/ to sign up!

By joining my mailing list, you'll also get exclusive news, specials, and access to my private VIP reader library.

ACKNOWLEDGMENTS

I've been putting off writing acknowledgments for the last volume of the *Toccata* series, I guess because I know when I write them this trilogy will be well and truly finished. It's been such an adventure to get this project together, and I've enjoyed every moment. Even on this story, which required I make the blood sacrifice of ripping my heart out of my chest and stomping on it repeatedly before agreeing to take the shape of a book.

The following folks deserve a world of thanks for their help along the way:

I'm indebted to my talented editor, Lynn O'Connacht, without whom *Prodigal Storm* would not have made it to the world before 2020. Lynn's got an unparalleled eye for story, and while they never hesitate to point out where change needs to happen, they've also been my staunch cheerleader. I couldn't have asked for a better collaborator. For the thoughtful discussions, the story ideas, and the good strong pushes, I'm grateful.

To Sara Rauch, whose weekly check-ins keep me on task and in my right mind (mostly);

To my writing group: Stephanie Eding, Leigh Landry, Maria Z. Medina, and Chace Verity, for whom most of the *Toccata System* planets are named (except Orthos...I had to throw a little Dumas in there);

To Killian Czuba, Jessie Kwak, and Sara Seyfarth, for your ongoing support, guidance, and friendship;

To my parents, who always believe;

To my sisters, Susan and Shana, who are thankfully NOT assassins and therefore won the dedication of this book;

To Milo, who's a silly monkey;

And to Moshe, who helps with everything, all the time, and seems to get calmer whenever I grow frantic.

Thanks, all! And now...on to the next! :)

ABOUT THE AUTHOR

Kate Sheeran Swed loves hot chocolate, plastic dinosaurs, and airplane tickets. She has trekked along the Inca Trail to Macchu Picchu, hiked on the Mýrdalsjökull glacier in Iceland, and climbed the ruins of Masada to watch the sunrise over the Dead Sea. Kate currently lives in New York's capital region with her husband and son, and two cats who were named after movie dogs (Benji and Beethoven). She holds an MFA in Fiction from Pacific University.

You can find more of Kate's work, and pick up a free short story collection, at katesheeranswed.com.

facebook.com/katesheeranswed

twitter.com/katesheeranswed

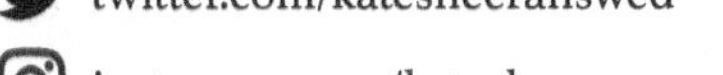
instagram.com/katesheeranswed